FURTHERMORE

AN ANTHOLOGY

REBEKAH CAMPBELL * DAVID ESTES
AMBER GARR * KAREN AMANDA HOOPER
STEPHANIE JUDICE * LEIGH MICHAEL

*For my dear friend, Brooke! Thank you for your unwavering support and encouragement.
Love, Stephanie Judice*

Furthermore: An Anthology

by

Rebekah Campbell
David Estes
Amber Garr
Karen Amanda Hooper
Stephanie Judice
Leigh Michael

"Surprise Visitor" Copyright © 2012 Rebekah Cambell
"Getting To Know the Heavies" Copyright © 2012 Rebekah Cambell
"People Change" Copyright © 2012 Rebekah Cambell
"The Runaway - Tawni's Story" Copyright © 2012 David Estes
"The Life Lottery - A Story from Year Zero" Copyright © 2012 David Estes
"Cold Feet" Copyright © 2012 Amber Garr
"Rift" Copyright © 2012 Amber Garr
"Discovery" Copyright © 2012 Amber Garr
"Human Resources" Copyright © 2012 Amber Garr
"The Sound of Love" Copyright © 2012 Karen Amanda Hooper
"Muirne's Melody" Copyright © 2012 Stephanie Judice
"Jeremy's Heart" Copyright © 2012 Stephanie Judice
"Fall From Grace" Copyright © 2012 Stephanie Judice
"Fate" Copyright © 2012 Leigh Michael

This is a work of fiction. The names, characters, places, and incidents are products of the author's imagination or have been used fictitiously and are not to be construed as real. Any resemblance to actual persons, living or dead, events, or locales is entirely coincidental.

All rights are reserved. No part of this book may be used or reproduced in any manner whatsoever without written permission from the authors.

Cover Art by Claudia at Phatpuppy Art (phatpuupyart.com)
Cover Design by Alexandra Shostak (alexandrashostak.wordpress.com)

ISBN-13: 978-1481006019
ISBN-10: 1481006010

A FEW WORDS

Cancer. The statistics are astounding and this disease has touched the lives of too many. I always felt like I wasn't doing enough to help the fight, so I decided to fix that.

After dreaming up this idea, I was excited to see so many others jump on board in a relatively short amount of time. I'd like to thank my fellow authors for contributing their excellent stories. I'm honored to be a part of this group. Likewise I am grateful for Claudia at Phatpuppy Art, who donated the cover art without hesitation and for Alexandra Shostak, who completed the design in honor of the cause.

So, thank you everyone, for being such amazing beings and for believing that we can make a difference.

~Amber

This anthology is dedicated to those who lost the battle and those who continue to fight.

AN ANTHOLOGY

CONTENTS

Surprise Visitor *Rebekah Cambell*	9
Getting To Know the Heavies *Rebekah Campbell*	19
People Change *Rebekah Cambell*	27
The Runaway - Tawni's Story *David Estes*	43
The Life Lottery - A Story from Year Zero *David Estes*	65
Cold Feet *Amber Garr*	79
Rift *Amber Garr*	91
Discovery *Amber Garr*	105
Human Resources *Amber Garr*	111
The Sound of Love *Karen Amanda Hooper*	121
Muirne's Melody *Stephanie Judice*	135
Jeremy's Heart *Stephanie Judice*	157
Fall From Grace *Stephanie Judice*	171
Fate *Leigh Michael*	183

AN ANTHOLOGY

All in a Day's Work

As part of The Darkness Through the Light Series

Rebekah Campbell

Surprise Visitor

While it seems as though everything is crumbling around her, Emily can still see glimmers of light. One particular glimmer takes the form of her hot best-friend-turned-boyfriend, Eric Baker. Unfortunately, Emily's suspension from school leaves her with a lot of time to fill. What she doesn't realize is that today is about to fill up quite nicely.

Getting to Know the Heavies

Normally, you will find the two Sullivan bodyguards running errands for their intimidating employer, leaving destruction and pain in their wake. But Miles and Tai are still human beings underneath it all. And everyone has a weakness.

People Change

Dennis Baker has spent the last thirteen years trying to raise his son the best way that he can. When Eric asks him a question about his mother, it's time to go back to where it all began and then went so badly wrong.

For the fighters who hold a place in our heart.

AN ANTHOLOGY

Surprise Visitor

Mornings. I used to dread mornings. Then again, I used to walk into the kitchen only to be met by a grimacing, overweight tyrant. This morning, I knew the empty kitchen would greet me, welcome me and remind me. He's not here anymore, Uncle Norman isn't coming back. Late nights would no longer be spent in front of the bathroom mirror, crying and shaking, as I pieced myself back together. I didn't need to look over my shoulder just in case his temper turned. The thick tension that forced itself into every inch of this cage-like home would eventually dissipate, allowing me to finally breathe.

This morning, I'd jumped out of bed. I didn't roll or fall out of bed as I normally did, today was different. I woke up a new girl. A smile tugged at the corners of my mouth, I rubbed the sleep out of my eyes, and embraced the happiness surging through my veins. Eric had told me he loved me. Eric told me that he loves – wait for it – me! His lips lightly brushed mine as his strong arms wrapped around me. The breath hitched in my chest as I remembered the way he pulled me so close to him that my heartbeat stuttered and I threw my arms around him. Dignity be damned.

The doorbell brought me back down from the clouds and my eyes flashed to the clock beside my bed. 10.00am. School already started so I knew it couldn't be Eric. The postman never rang the doorbell either. He just forced everything through the letterbox no matter the size. Uncle Norman had taken his rage out on me more than once because of that damn postie.

I pulled my thin, beige curtains to the side and squinted past the glare of the sun to try and catch a glance of the random visitor. Brown, tousled hair. Tall with broad shoulders. Blue T-shirt that clung to all the right places, my stomach swirled as I realised who it could be. Then he looked up to my window and I crushed the curtain back in to place.

"Crap, it's Eric!" I said to the empty room, heart hammering. My boyfriend had sprung a surprise visit on me and here I stood in my bedroom in Betty Boop pyjamas and a serious case of bedhead. Thankful for my messy ways, I grabbed a discarded pair of jeans from the floor and dragged them on. A plain black jumper hung on the back of my door and I pulled it over my head as I did up the zip on my jeans with one hand.

I'd started walking along the corridor when I caught a glimpse of myself in the bathroom mirror. My brown hair had frizzed and foofed itself in to another dimension. Love or not, I wasn't going to let Eric see me like this.

I growled in frustration as ran back to my bedroom and kicked at the scattered piles on the floor looking for a hair bobble. I knew I had enough bobbles to drown in but it now seemed like I was in the middle of a drought. I kicked another pile and a black hat flew across the room.

I chased after it and thrust it on my head, tucking strands of my hair underneath the band of it. "It'll have to do," I mumbled as I walked back along the corridor, my reflection no longer resembling that of the Bride of Frankenstein.

The old staircase creaked and groaned as I thundered down it towards the front door. My cheeks flushed as I put my hand on the doorknob. My boyfriend was on the other side of the door and I looked like an electrocuted tomato. Maybe I would be overcome by a wave of wit and charm and he would be too dazzled to notice? Or maybe he would run away in horror?

I bit the bullet and opened the door. With a chiselled jaw, deep brown eyes and a smile that could make a Southern Belle swoon: Eric was definitely a sight for sore eyes.

"Good morning," he said. Oh that voice of his. So smooth and rich – music to my ears.

"Good morning," I smiled. At least my brain was working. His eyes glinted as he leaned forward and gave me the sweetest, lightest of kisses. A sudden thought struck me – I hadn't had time to brush my teeth.

I leaned away from him and disrupted the kiss before it had a chance to develop. His eyebrows crinkled but he didn't say anything as he moved back a step. The sun blazed over the top of his head and I held up a hand to shield my eyes from the searing rays.

"Shouldn't you be in school?" I asked.

His confusion turned into a mischievous grin. "I thought I would skive off and take my girlfriend out for the day."

A thrill swam through me and I smiled back. "I guess I must be a bad influence then."

Eric frowned and dug his hands in his jeans pockets. "What do you mean?"

"Suspended for a week and encouraging you to take the day off too."

"Emily Jenkins, corrupting young men. What would people say?" He tutted at me and as if by magic, I spotted an elderly lady walking along the pavement, scrunching up her nose to stare at us.

I looked away from her to take in the handsome, cheeky devil in front of me. "The young man didn't take much corrupting?"

Eric shook his head slowly. "You're wrong there. They'll say the young man was a pillar of the community and he just couldn't resist those baby blues."

"I'm guessing your dad couldn't resist your puppy eyes either. How did you convince him to let you off?"

"He's a complete pushover."

I quirked an eyebrow, a trick that had taken me a good fifteen minutes to master and one that I took every opportunity to use.

Eric rolled his brown eyes. "Fine, I used the water trick." He took a step forward, disrupting the furious sun's view.

"The water trick?" I folded my arms and realised with horror that I'd forgotten to put a bra on. I thanked my lucky stars that the shadowy hallway had hidden it from Eric. What a looker I am, hair like a wild animal, breath more deadly than a cobra, and no bra.

"Yeah, I went to the bathroom with a glass of water and pretended to be sick while I poured the water down the toilet."

My mouth dropped open. "That is genius!" Why had I never thought of that before?

"You should know that already, Em." Eric brought his right hand up to his face, blew on the nails and then rubbed them on his chest. My attention focused on the muscle in his arm that flexed and bulged as he did it, it wouldn't do to stare.

"You sure think a lot of yourself, Baker. Well if we're going out, do you want to come in and wait while I get ready?" I nudged the front door wide open with my foot as I kept my arms folded tightly against my chest.

He gestured towards me. "You're already dressed though."

"I'm dressed but I'm not ready." He stepped inside and the smell of coffee and Calvin Klein brushed past me. My blood hummed as he walked through to the living room and sat on the couch. I desperately wanted to join him and spend all day cuddled in his lap watching ridiculous daytime television.

No, we were going on our first date. No time for canoodling on the sofa.

Of course, there was always time for other types of canoodling. My mind screamed *Get back on track, Emily!*

"So what shall I wear?"

Eric's eyebrows rose and I realised what a stupid question it was. "What you're wearing looks good to me."

"I can't wear this so what will we be doing?"

He tapped his index finger against his nose and winked. "It's a surprise."

"Give me a clue," I whined. I hated surprises and Eric knew it, we'd been best friends for ten years after all.

"Well it'll be cold so you might want to wrap up a little."

I looked at him in his tight T-shirt and frowned. "Won't you be cold if that's the case?"

"No, I've got a jacket waiting for me so stop stalling and get changed. We have a bus to catch."

***

After I'd brushed my hair, changed into some clean clothes, and brushed my teeth, I resembled a normal human being that could venture outside without the threat of an angry mob. The thick blue jumper drew attention to my eyes and draped over the top of my dark hip-hugging jeans.

Eric's fingers laced with mine as we got off the bus and started to walk along the riverbank. The crisp leaves scuffed under our feet and I took in the unmistakeable smell of autumn. It was a clean, almost perfectly created woody scent that faintly nipped at my nose. It hinted that snow was just around the corner, a sly warning that winter would soon reclaim the world with a pure blanket.

I shivered and nudged Eric with my shoulder. "Are you going to give me any clues?"

He shook his head in response and I used my other hand to rub the hollow of his elbow. "Well can I throw some guesses out there and you can tell me if I'm right?"

"Okay, but I'm not going to tell you if I think it might ruin the surprise. And don't go thinking that doing that to my arm will make me spill the beans." I flashed a smile at him and Eric grinned back, squeezing my hand a little with his. I glanced around to take in the flowing river and the white footbridge that I knew lurked around the corner.

"Are we going to the Islands?" The Islands were exactly that: two tiny connected islands in the middle of the river. Walking through the islands to the other side of the river was like walking through a fairytale. Tall majestic trees flagged you on both sides as you walked through the brush of what could easily be mistaken for a forest floor. I could picture the woodland creatures that lurked around every corner: a skittish rabbit snuffling through the clover and the family of birds that sang of the enchantment surrounding me. I loved the Islands.

"No, we're not going to the Islands. Not today anyway."

Keep brainstorming, Emily. "You said it'd be cold so are we going on some kind of weird hill walk?"

Eric sighed and looked at me as if I was a moron. "So you could complain the whole way up the hill and the whole way back? No, we're not going hill walking. I think you forget that I know you better than you know yourself."

"Phew. You had me worried there for a second." If what he said were true, he wouldn't be here with me. Eric would be far away from me, living with the knowledge that he can't save everyone, especially me. I leaned my head on his shoulder and tried to tell myself that it might not always be this way. The memory of Uncle Norman would fade and maybe Eric could come to understand why I did what I did.

Of course, that all depended on me breaking down my barrier's that kept him blissfully ignorant.

We carried on walking along the river as the sparrows darted through the trees and a seagull cawed in the distance.

Eric eventually sighed and said. "It does kind of involve exercise though. That's the only clue you're getting."

A bland rectangular building crept out from behind the greenery on the left hand side. Eric tugged on my hand and we crossed the road towards it.

"Ice Skating? You do realise that my clumsy gene goes into overdrive on a slippery surface, don't you?"

He chuckled at me. "It's okay, I'll catch you, Em. Failing that, I know First Aid. In fact, you look a little breathless at the moment, maybe the kiss of life will sort you out?" Eric leaned down towards me.

I held my hand out to his mouth and shook my head. "I'm afraid that I'll have to reserve judgment on that until I see this surprise."

"Wow, we've only been going out for a day and I've already been denied. I suppose I'll forgive you when you're showering me with kisses after we walk through that door."

I pulled my hand out of his and shoved him with all of my strength. Eric staggered to the side and I raced along the pavement towards the blue door.

"Hey! No fair!" He yelled at me as I heard him sprinting after me. The air burned in my lungs as I yelled back "All is fair in love and surprises, Baker!" My steps faltered as I hauled open the blue door and passed through the darkness. A light flashed through the window of the door ahead of me. Eric burst through after me and slammed a hand on the door frame as I reached for the handle.

"Just...wait...always in a rush," he eventually managed through ragged breaths. The thought that there was something waiting for me on the other side of that had my stomach doing somersaults.

My mouth ran dry and I hopped on both feet. "Come on, Eric! I hate surprises, just open the door."

The crooked smile that I loved so much swept across his face and he leaned against the wall beside the door, crossing his arms. "Open it."

I narrowed my eyes at him and yanked open the door, only to be met with a sight that had the breath gushing out of my lungs.

***

Her jaw dropped open and her blue eyes stared at the ice rink. If I'd been standing behind her, I would have been compelled to do an air grab in celebration. However, in the unwritten boyfriend code, it was a definite no-no to do it right in front of her.

In the middle of the ice rink was a table and two chairs, and standing beside them was the new guy, Isaac. He was kitted out in a white shirt and black trousers and in his hands were a bouquet of flowers. I'd spent an hour in the flower shop this morning trying to pick the perfect bunch and once I'd finally decided, the florist had told me all of their names. All I knew was that there were a couple of red ones, some dark blue ones and white fluffy stuff in there somewhere.

Emily gleamed in the strobe lights that waltzed across the walls and her jaw still hung open. I gave myself a mental pat on the back and smiled down at her, all of that last minute rushing about had been worth it. Anything would have been worth it to see this look on her face. A small smile played at the corners of her mouth, it added to the astonished expression. No, it didn't add to it, it moulded the expression into one of pure, unadulterated happiness. I had made her happy.

Emily reached out for my hand and I pushed away from the wall to lead her through the doorway. The fairy lights wrapped around the top of the rink cast a purple glow on the immaculate ice with a thick black strip of carpet that stretched from the edge to the table.

I wrapped an arm around her shoulders and kissed the top of her head softly, looking out on to the ice. "Come on then, princess. I've waited ten years to call you my girlfriend so it's about time we had our first date."

Getting to Know the Heavies

The two bodyguards couldn't be more opposite if they tried. Miles had jet black hair with flashes of grey woven throughout. Tai had none. He preferred the bald, dangerously scary look.

As lean as a beanpole, the way Miles carried himself warned you not to cross him. Tai was also tall but he had muscles upon muscles. His thick build left you with no doubt that he could rip you limb from limb without breaking a sweat.

However, the biggest difference was in their eyes.

Miles' dead, green eyes dragged across every inch of a room, taking in each little detail, but the slightest movement would bring them snapping back to attention. Only the bravest–or most stupid–individuals dared to look into his eyes. In their murky depths, you would find shadows of every terrible deed he'd carried out. Look even closer and you might see the worst nightmares you were yet to have.

Tai had hazel brown eyes that darted around the room like flashes of lightning. Tiny sparks of mischief were always glinting, enticing, capturing. At the moment, however, the only glistening, enticing, and capturing was coming from two luscious cupcakes.

In the vast kitchen of the Sullivan home, Miles scrubbed the droplets of blood from his weathered hands over the deep sink. Tai had seated himself upon a sturdy metal chair at the island and gawped at the two mouth-watering creations on a plate in front of him.

"Do you think they're for us?"

The water shut off and Miles turned to face his burly partner. As a man of few words, he simply shrugged and jutted out his lower lip, a move that drew attention to the jagged scar etched on his cheek.

"You're right. Who would buy us cupcakes?" Tai tucked a clenched fist under his chin and continued staring.

"Miss Sullivan is not above bribery," Miles said.

"I should hope not," an Irish voice echoed from the doorway.

Tai stumbled off the stool and buttoned his black suit jacket. "Mr. Sullivan." The two bodyguards nodded in unison.

The brown haired employer moved a couple of steps towards them. Silver S's decorated the cuffs of his royal blue shirt. Everything about the man screamed power: from his perfectly trimmed goatee to the polished black leather shoes that adorned his feet. "Did you do as I asked, gentlemen?" The heavy tone lay thick in the air.

Miles answered. "Yes, sir. We have passed your regards on to Mr. Morgan."

"Good," he said. "In that case, can I ask why Tai is drooling over a cupcake?"

Tai's chiselled cheeks glowed a bright shade of pink and he cleared his throat. "I have a bit of a sweet tooth, Mr. Sullivan."

"Is that so? I assumed you were a grind-up-their-bones kind of man."

A sly smile crept across the bodyguard's face. "Sorry, sir, but have we climbed up a beanstalk?"

Michael Sullivan laughed and moved closer to Tai, his expensive shoes providing an ominous clicking noise. It was a dangerous laugh, erring on the side of manic. Miles motioned to Tai sharply across his throat with his right hand. The burly man ignored his mentor's warning and started to laugh with Michael.

"That's funny. It must be your sense of humour that made me hire you, Tai." The laugh cut off in his throat and was replaced with venom. "No, wait, it was your ability to take down a man before he has the chance to see his life flash before his eyes." Michael Sullivan was now dangerously hovering in Tai's personal space but the bodyguard felt that *he* was the intimidated one. Grey eyes bore into him, narrowing and flaring all at once.

"Miles obviously hasn't shown you the ropes so I'll give you a tip. I tell the jokes here. Got that, Chuckles?" Tai nodded and tried to fight the overwhelming urge to gulp.

"Daddy?" a red haired girl edged forward in to the kitchen. She cautiously glanced around the room. Taking in her father's furious state and Tai trying to crush himself against the wall, she sighed and shook her head. "What did he do, Miles?"

"He made a joke, Miss Sullivan."

Carrie held a hand to her forehead and shook it slowly. "Tai's a moron, Daddy. Think of the time it'd take you to find a replacement if you kill him."

Michael tore his blazing eyes away and focused them on his daughter. His jaw unclenched and the fire in his eyes dimmed, cinder by cinder. With a muscle tensing in his jaw, he stepped back and straightened his own tie. "Oh, Caroline, I wouldn't kill Tai."

He started to laugh again and Tai nervously joined him. Michael walked towards the hallway, tucked his hands into his pockets and, still laughing, said, "I'd get Miles to do it."

Tai's bulky head twisted towards his mentor who simply shrugged his shoulders.

***

"You're not very concerned about your own self-preservation are you, Tai?" Carrie sat herself on the worktop and licked the white icing off one of the cupcakes. He had managed to find out the cupcakes were in fact a present from Mrs. Sullivan.

"I spent the majority of my childhood squaring up to the other kids in the playground. My self-preservation dial may be a lot lower than yours, Miss Sullivan," he replied as he tried not to drool.

"What was your latest job anyway?"

The two men shared a quick glance and Miles shook his head. He continued leaning back against the sink but Carrie didn't pay any attention to him. Over the course of her sixteen years, she would've learned that trying to get information out of Miles was like trying to squeeze blood out of a stone.

"You know we aren't allowed to tell you that," Tai said. The girl sighed and started to break up the cupcakes with her fingers. The look on the bodyguard's face didn't go unnoticed.

"This cupcake is amazing, I wonder who I should give the last one to." She popped some crumbs into her mouth and smiled at Tai. Miles took his cue and moved away from the sink, limping slightly as he always did, to stand beside his partner.

"Miss Sullivan, sweet smiles don't become you."

Carrie cocked her head to the side and plastered an innocent look on her face. "Why ever not, Miles?"

"Appearances are always deceptive within this household."

She narrowed her eyes at the lanky man. "Well at least I know Miles isn't getting a cupcake." Carrie looked at Tai again. "Tell me, Tai, how can you stand working with someone as grumpy as him?"

Tai cleared his throat and looked to his mentor who still watched Carrie carefully.

"I wouldn't say that Miles is grumpy, he's just good at his job. The guy knows when he needs to keep his mouth shut and blend into the background."

Miles mouth tugged a little at the corners but he was not a man that ever smiled. His face returned to its blank and steely, slightly creepy normal state.

Carrie licked her fingers and tried to stare down the ominous bodyguard but she knew better. "Looks like you haven't grasped that then, Tai." She turned her attention back to the brute.

"My skills lay elsewhere, Miss Sullivan," he said.

Carrie crumpled up the cupcake case and dropped it on the counter in a pile of crumbs. "Good thing too, I have a job for you, both of you."

Tai stood up from his chair and brushed the creases out of his suit jacket. "I hope it's not to do with that young girl from the summer."

"As a matter of fact it is."

His forehead creased and his mouth drew into a thin white line. "Hasn't she had enough?"

Carrie hopped down from the counter and stuck her hands on her hips. "When did you develop a conscience? She needs to be put in her place. Don't make me go and tell Daddy that his bodyguard's gone soft. He really will make Miles kill you then." Tai stayed silent and let out a deep breath through his nose.

"That's what I thought. Come with me, I'd rather run the idea past you first. Unless it's going to bother your poor conscience?"

***

Fifteen minutes later, Tai stormed into the kitchen as Miles tucked a metal stool back under the counter and cleared away a plate. Tai cracked his knuckles, a scowl plastered on his face. Miles watched him carefully and then sighed. "Why does the Emily Jenkins situation bother you so much?"

"I'm not bothered."

"Oh really? Is that why you're wearing a hole in the lino?"

Tai stopped pacing and pulled the metal stool back out, seated himself on it, and tapped his foot against the side.

Miles crossed his arms across his chest. "It intrigues me. You're quite happy to beat up a school head teacher and there have been a number of Mr. Sullivan's work associates you have dealt with in the past. What is so different about a sixteen year old girl?"

Tai huffed and picked up Carrie's discarded cupcake case, scrunched it up some more and then tossed it into the kitchen bin. "I have an eleven year old niece, I was actually supposed to take her ice skating this afternoon but they'd closed it for some reason. Anyway, there's nothing I wouldn't do for Lydia. I would hate for her to go through the same thing that Miss Sullivan put the Emily girl through. I'd want to find the person responsible and make them suffer until they begged. Their blood could be spilling over the cobbles and it still wouldn't be enough." A vein pulsated at the side of his neck, causing the thick, black tribal tattoo to twitch above the collar of his white shirt.

"I can understand that," Miles whispered. Tai looked over and saw the forlorn look on his face.

"You can?"

Miles scoffed at him. "I'm not the heartless zombie that others believe I am." He zoned out for a few seconds before he said "What's the plan?"

"I managed to turn Miss Sullivan's attention to someone other than Emily but you'd better have your game face on tomorrow, Miles, it's going to be a heavy duty job. Maybe eat some spinach or something, see if you can go all Popeye on me. Speaking of food....where's the cupcake?" His brown eyes roved over the counter and eventually alighted on the empty plate by the sink.

"They weren't for us. Mrs. Sullivan came back for it." Miles shrugged his shoulder and moved a little further from his colleague. Tai's eyes wandered over him and a small smile took hold, mischief glinted in his eyes.

He took in a deep breath and stood up from the chair, shoving it under the island with a clang. "You know what I admire about you, Miles?" The lean man looked confused for a second. "It's your honesty. Do you know how difficult it is to meet anyone truly honest? Someone who will tell it to you straight?" Tai stepped towards Miles and started to dust at the shoulders of the man's suit. "I know that if push came to shove, you would never lie to me, Miles. You're a true friend."

Tai's hands brushed the left lapel of Miles' jacket and the thin man narrowed his eyes carefully. Tai simply grinned at him and said, "Just a couple of crumbs."

People Change

Eric burst into the living room and threw himself down beside me on the couch. When my cup of tea lurched and spilled over the brim, I thrust my arm forward to avoid third degree burns. "Easy, tiger! I'm guessing it went well then?"

"It was awesome. She was totally gobsmacked, I just wish I'd thought to take a camera with me." He let out a happy sigh and I chuckled at him, the soppy rascal.

"Yeah, surprising Emily is a rare occurrence so you probably should have taken advantage."

"Seriously, dad, I don't think I've ever seen her so happy before. It's kind of refreshing, you know?"

After Emily's accident, she'd gone through a drastic transformation. Once a shy and retiring wallflower, to say she'd changed would be an understatement. Emily wouldn't have looked at someone in the wrong way, yet now she'd been suspended from school for attacking another girl. "Well, I'm really pleased that you had such a great first date."

He looked at me with his thinking face. Mouth scrunched to the side and eyes narrowed, I knew what was coming. "Dad? Where did you take my Mam on your first date?"

I heaved myself off the couch and took the half-empty cup over to the kitchen counter.

"It's just that you've never told me before and I'm curious." He followed me over to the kitchen area and pulled up a stool at the breakfast bar.

"I never told you because we don't normally talk about her." I balanced a new teabag on a teaspoon and held it over the cup.

"Why not?"

The water from the kettle splashed over the teabag turning the milky liquid darker. "I suppose it's because she left. There's no point dwelling on the past when all you can change is the future." I set the kettle back on its stand and sighed.

"Wow. That's pretty deep for an old man." Eric ducked just in time as I swiped towards him with my free hand.

"Cheeky brat." I picked up another mug from the draining board and held it towards him. "Want one? I can just use the same teabag if you do?"

Eric nodded back at me. "Yeah sure. Now come on old timer, spill the beans. Was it a really cheesy first date? I bet you cried like the time we watched *The Hunger Games*." Eric winked at me.

"I didn't cry. My eyes were sweaty."

He crooked an eyebrow at me. "Oh really? I thought you said it was because you were drowning a fly."

"I *was* drowning a fly…because my eyes were sweaty. Now are you going to shut up or shall I keep it to myself?"

Eric held up his hands and slid off the chair as I passed the full mug towards him. "So where did you take her? The cinema? Out for dinner?"

I cringed inside. I knew that telling Eric would give him permission to take the mick out of me every chance he could.

I sighed. "Technically, it was the café in Accident and Emergency. What are you doing?"

Eric had set his tea back on the counter and was now rifling through the cupboard next to the fridge. "I'm going to need some biscuits for this. Possibly popcorn as well." He brought a packet of chocolate hobnobs from the back of the cupboard and grinned at me as he picked up his mug and walked back towards the couch with them.

"Well, don't be greedy with them. I'll need a couple of those to get through the winter." I sat down on the couch next to my son and he turned to me with that disappointed look he somehow managed to pull off even better than I did. And who was meant to be the parent here?

"Dad, with that beer belly you're brewing up, I seriously doubt you'll die of starvation. Stop trying to change the subject and tell me the freaking story!"

"Fine, fine. I was waiting for a taxi…"

The rain soaked through my jacket and plastered the hair to my face. Every few seconds, drops would break free and streak down into my eyes. The only thing that hurt more than the biting wind was the fact that it was my own fault.

If I'd changed the oil like I kept meaning to do then the car wouldn't have died and I wouldn't be waiting at an empty taxi rank trying to get to work.

Standing at the taxi rank on a Tuesday morning meant that I got to watch as people swanned by with their massive umbrellas or drove past in their toasty cars. My socks squelched as I started to shift on both feet, trying to get any kind of warmth through my body.

Heels clattered through the sound of rain drops and I turned my head to greet my fellow miserable companion.

My chest twisted and pulsed as my heart tried to break through my ribs. Blimey, if I lost my sight, at least I had this vision to lead me through eternity. She was a muse, a goddess, a total fox.

She was beautiful.

Her deep brown eyes glittered as she smiled at me from underneath her pink umbrella. Chocolate coloured hair wrapped up into a bun apart from a fringe that swept across her forehead.

"Horrible weather isn't it?"

Wait a minute, she was speaking to me. *Answer her man!* "Yeah."

Smooth, real smooth.

"How long have you been waiting?" she asked. Her thick eyelashes blinked at me, and my brain slowly started to work again. I looked at my watch on what was turning into a very red, icy left hand.

"About ten minutes?"

"Oh." She noticed my jaw chattering in the cold. "Want to share my umbrella? I know you're already drenched but–"

I dove under the umbrella and smiled at her. "Sorry, that was a bit creepy wasn't it?"

She smirked at me. "A little bit, yeah. Then again, I did ask."

I cleared my throat and rocked back on my heels before offering my hand to her. "Well, seeing as I threw myself into your personal space, I suppose the polite thing to do is to introduce myself. I'm Dennis."

She hesitated a moment before extending a purple knitted glove and shaking my hand. "I'm Jill. Nice to meet you, Dennis."

A gust of wind swept underneath the umbrella and she pulled her grey coat closer around her neck. Her perfume washed over me: a mix of sherbet, coconuts and coffee. I kept my mouth tightly closed, if I drooled on her then I could kiss goodbye any future conversation.

The cold gnawed at my fingers so I cupped them around my mouth and blew hot air into them. If I kept breathing on them then I may only lose one or two.

"I might have a spare pair of gloves if you'd like to borrow them?" Jill shrugged off her handbag and delved about inside before producing a pink pair to match the umbrella.

"That's really nice of you but I'm afraid my testosterone levels can only take so much. The pink umbrella is pushing the limit as it is, thank you though." I pointed up at the pink hue surrounding us and she laughed at me.

"Suit yourself." She tucked the gloves into her handbag and placed it back on her shoulder. I watched as she glanced at her wrist before leaning out towards the road and gazing up to the corner.

"Running late?"

"Dentist appointment. You?"

"Work."

"Oh no! When are you supposed to start?"

"Probably about now."

Her mouth dropped open and she crossed her arms as another gust of wind flew around us. "Do you think you'll get in trouble?"

I shook my head and rubbed my hands together. "No, I don't think so. I just started working for my father a couple of weeks ago so he should let me off. Hey, look." I pointed past her at the car coming round the corner with a glowing beacon on the roof.

"You take this one, Jill. There should be another coming any minute."

She looked up at me with those dark eyes. "No, you're already late for work. I'll be okay, you can take this one."

The car pulled up in front of us and I opened the back door for her. "No, I insist. You have a dentist appointment. I know how full their diaries can be so you go ahead." She chewed on her bottom lip and glanced from me to the taxi and back again.

The taxi driver bellowed from the front seat. "Someone get in the bloody car, you're letting all the heat out."

That sold it for her. She closed up the umbrella and ducked inside as the rain began its descent on my damp clothes. Jill looked up at me from the seat as I wrapped my hand around the door. "Thank you, Dennis. That's really kind of you."

"You're welcome. It's nice to meet you, Jill." She smiled brightly at me and I started to close the door.

Before I knew it, blessed heat shot up my arm. Only it wasn't blessed heat, it was bloody painful! I wanted the cold back, please let me have the cold back. I looked at the taxi and saw that my fingers were trapped in the door. Panic set in and I started to pound on the roof of the taxi before it had a chance to drive off. I would rather hop about like a madman than be dragged along the high street by my fingers.

The door opened and I pulled my throbbing fingers out from the door well. A rainbow of swear words spewed out of my mouth as the pain intensified. I squeezed my fingers together in a desperate attempt to stem the blood flow as I crumpled to my knees on the sodden pavement.

"Oh hell, Dennis! Are you okay?"

I wanted to tell her that it felt like my hand had been stuck in a blender. I also wanted to ask her to check if my fingernails and dignity were in the door well.

Instead I mumbled a strained "Never better," and silently prayed for death. Her arms brushed around my shoulders and she gently coaxed my injured hand away from my chest.

"I'm sorry, Dennis. I'm so sorry, I don't know what happened. I think, oh, I think you need to go to the hospital." Her voice drifted off the end of the sentence and my eyes pried open to look at the devastation.

My fingernails had turned a deep purple that rivalled her knitted gloves and the gashes along the creases of my finger joints reminded me of train tracks. Very bloody train tracks. A white line that looked almost like chalk etched its way beneath my knuckles.

"It's just a scratch, I'll be fine. You better leave if you want to make your appointment." I gave her what I hoped looked like a brave smile.

"Stuff the appointment, I'm taking you to the hospital." She paused and then inspected my face. "Dennis, are you crying?"

"There's a fly in my eye, just trying to drown it, that's all."

***

Walking into Accident and Emergency was like walking into a zoo. A four-year-old boy with a yellow toy car stuffed up his nose cried for his mam. Across from him was an elderly lady with a broken pair of glasses in one hand, holding a used-to-be-white tissue to the side of her eye. Sat next to her was a young woman who'd propped one very swollen foot onto the seat beside her. As always, there was a drunk in the corner having a very lovely conversation with the water cooler.

"You gave such a good sermon," he mumbled and gestured to the stray bubbles that floated to the top.

"Dennis? Do you want to get yourself checked in while I find something for your hand?" I looked back at Jill, her immaculate styled hair had started to disentangle itself, perfectly framing her face. She cleared her throat and the sparkling brown eyes scanned mine. Crap, was I supposed to answer?

"Yeah sure."

The receptionist at the desk watched me with beady eyes as I cautiously walked up to her window. Her short, white hair stuck out at all angles and her mouth formed a grim line.

"Name and date of birth," she snapped.

"Good morning to you, too."

"Name and date of birth."

"Yes, it is a bit miserable today, isn't it?"

She sighed and the look she gave me could have killed a goat. "I don't have time for this."

"Name and date of birth?" I offered. She nodded in reply and her eyes flitted back to the computer screen in front of her. "Dennis Baker. Tenth of July 1970."

Jill re-appeared by my side with a pad of wet toilet roll. "Sorry, this was all I could find. I thought I'd better wet it so you could try cleaning it out."

The throbbing in my hand sped up a notch at the thought of placing something freezing cold near the hot skin.

"Reason for your visit today," the receptionist butted in.

Jill started to open her mouth but I held up a finger and leaned further towards the window. "I was viciously assaulted by a young woman with a pink umbrella."

She laughed and batted my arm. "See? She's unstable!"

***

The door to my son's bedroom had been left open just a crack but it was enough for me to watch the last time he had a conversation with his mother. "Eric, come here, come and sit on my knee." Jill held her hands out to the curly-haired boy wonder. He clutched a train to his side and walked towards her. She scooped him up and sat him on her knees.

"Mammy? Can we play with my trains now?"

"I can't, darling. I've got to go soon."

He scrunched up his face and tore his attention from the bright, red train. "Go where?" His eyes lit up and a smile plastered on his face. "Are we going to the park?"

"No, we're not going to the park. Mammy has to go somewhere by herself. I'm going to find my own house and you're staying here with Daddy until I find one you'll like."

His three-year-old face went back to being confused. "What's wrong with our house?"

She smiled at him and stroked his hair. "Nothing's wrong with the house, I just can't live here anymore."

"But why?"

She tried to speak but stopped. I watched as Jill struggled to find the words, desperate to rush in and tell her that there was a simple solution. Stay.

She cleared her throat and said, "Me and Daddy aren't getting on very well now so it's best for you if I find another house."

"What about me? Can I come too?"

She kissed the side of his head and I saw the stray tear drop onto Eric's downy hair. "No, darling. You're going to stay here with Daddy."

He tucked his chin in and started fiddling with the wheel on his train. "But I don't want you to go."

"I have to, but I'll come back to see you once I'm settled."

Eric scrabbled up to kneel on her lap and held his hand out to her. "You have to promise. Remember, you can't break a pinky promise."

It got too much for me. I moved away from the doorway and brushed a hand over my face. I couldn't watch the hope gleam in his face, seeing it crushed in the future would be tougher to handle. The door creaked open and I turned to see her wiping tears from her eyes.

She looked up and gave me a trembling smile. I dug my hands into my pockets, if they were free then they would reach for her. Being rejected by her would destroy me, I was sure of it. "You don't need to go, Jill. I'll sleep in Eric's room, you two can have our bed."

Jill shook her head and pushed past me. "You and I both know it wouldn't be fair to him. He doesn't need us arguing all the time. Besides, this will make it easier for you too."

"Don't be daft, I can look after myself, I can handle it, Jill."

"You think I actually want to leave? It's killing me that I can't feel the same way as you anymore. I *want* to be happy again, happy with you, but I can't. There's nothing between us now and you deserve to find someone who'll love you better than I could."

I shook my head and moved closer to her, hands still safely tucked away. "It might not be good enough for you but it is for me. Just stay with me, I need you."

"You say that now but it would change you in the future. You'd end up resenting me for not loving you and taking away the chance of finding someone else. Someone better." She sighed and walked along the corridor to her packed suitcase. Behind me, I could hear Eric mimicking explosions and the clatter of wheels colliding. "I'm sorry, Dennis. It's for the best. I'll call you when I get to my mam's and we'll work out a way for me to see Eric." Then she opened the front door and closed it quietly behind her. That was it? That was the end of my marriage? A suitcase and a closed door?

"Daddy?" Eric stood behind me, running his train up the doorframe and making a great show of watching it.

"Yes?"

"Will you play trains with me?" His tiny voice clutched at my chest and I struggled to maintain my composure. Her brown eyes looked up at me from his sweet face. I edged towards his door once more and scooped him into my arms, ignoring his squeals as I tickled his stomach.

I moved my hand to the back of his neck and set off even more irresistible giggles. "How about we play trains all day and then we can go and get some pizza?" I stopped long enough for him to shout a very enthusiastic "Yaaaaaaaaay!"

I had to make sure that I gave him enough love for the both of us now, people may change but love doesn't. Love is the constant.

ABOUT THE AUTHOR

In between working two different jobs, and confusing herself about which job she should be at, Rebekah manages to find the time to create new characters and worlds. Sleep is overrated. When she's not tapping away at her computer, you'll find Rebekah busting some moves to her favourite bands or setting up on the beach to have a bonfire with the best group of friends you could ask for.

Buy *Living in the Dark* on Amazon, Barnes and Noble, and Smashwords.

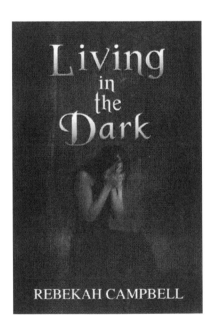

Learn more about Rebekah and her book at:
http://reflectivebookworm.blogspot.com
Follow Rebekah on Twitter @RBBookworm

AN ANTHOLOGY

Deeper - Two Tales from the Tri-Realms

David Estes

In *The Moon Dwellers*, Adele befriended an upbeat and unusual girl named Tawni, whose life was inexplicably linked to hers in ways she has only begun to understand. Wrongfully confined to a juvenile prison—the Pen—together, they began a journey of hope, friendship, and family that would change them both forever. But what happened to Tawni before being sent to the Pen? How did she end up in such an awful place? And why did she run from a life of privilege and luxury? Find out in the short story, *The Runaway- Tawni's Story*.

To my Goodreads Fan Group. You asked for more about Tawni, and you got it!

AN ANTHOLOGY

The Runaway - Tawni's Story

Even when you know it's the right thing to do, running away from home is never easy.

Although my small bag is packed and dangling from my shoulder, my nondescript black boots are laced, and the door is open, I linger on the threshold for a moment, and gaze back at the house I've called home for as long as I can remember. Everything I see—from the flat-screen telebox, to the sturdy stone table, to the photos of my parents and me hanging on the wall—should be familiar, but it's not. It's as if I've never seen any of it before. Ever since I overheard my parents talking last week, my entire world feels foreign.

I cannot wait any longer or I know I might change my mind. Swiping a long lock of straight, blond hair away from my face, I take a deep breath, close my eyes, and try to muster what little courage I can.

It's such a normal thing, stepping through the door, something I've done a million times. But this time it feels so *un*normal, like it's not me, not my legs—someone else. Not me. When I close it behind me I feel an errant rush of wind through the cave; it washes over my face, my arms, through my hair, as if the unlikely breeze is cleansing me, washing away the sins that are mine by association. Having left the house in which my parents are still sleeping, I feel cleaner already.

They're not good people. I can't stay here anymore.

With practiced steps I zigzag through the rock garden in our front yard. Most moon dwellers can't afford to waste perfectly good stones for decoration—but my parents are not most moon dwellers. Now that I know why my family is so wealthy amongst such poverty, seeing the polished and shiny stones makes me sick to my stomach.

It's still too early for the broad overhead cavern lights to be on, but I don't risk illuminating my flashlight for fear of drawing the attention of one of the Enforcers that roam our subchapter at all times. This deep below the earth's surface, we don't get much electricity anyway, so I'm used to seeing in the dark. But still, I take extra caution with each step, being careful not to stub my toe or kick a loose stone.

As I exit our walled-in property, I feel the pace of my heartbeat pick up. Although I'm walking slowly, my heart is racing. I might be walking, but in my heart I'm running away.

I'm running away.

I'm.

Running.

Away.

The words feel prickly in my mind and I wince as the dull throb of a headache starts in my left temple. I feel a trickle of sweat slide intimately down my back beneath my gray tunic. Ignoring the sweat, my racing heart, and the icy stab of the truest words I've ever thought in my head, I take another deep breath, reposition my shoulder satchel, and walk faster, stepping on the tips of my feet to remain as quiet as possible.

The night is quiet.

The neighborhood I grew up in, played in, made friends in, disappears beneath the soles of my boots, like the cool night air vanishes in the wake of the wings of a bat. With each step I gain strength in both my legs and my heart. Another suburban block slides away behind me.

My goal is to make it to the train station before the morning rush. Then, when the mass exodus of workers seeking work begins from our faltering subchapter, I might be able to blend into the crowds and escape the roving eyes of intra-Realm security. I bought my ticket in advance, which doesn't require an intra-Realm travel authorization; however, when I go through security I'll be required to provide my pass. Unfortunately, there's no way a sixteen-year-old girl would be granted such authorization, so I was forced to hurriedly purchase a cheap fake from a shady guy at school.

I hope it'll pass the scrutiny of the security guards.

Travelling intra-Realm without authorization is a serious offense that automatically requires time in the Pen, our local branch of the Moon Realm juvenile detention system. A lot of kids that go in there don't come out alive. My best friend, Cole, got sent there three months ago when an Enforcer tried to rape his sister. Cole killed the guy, but then his buddies killed Cole's sister and parents. They sent him to the Pen for life.

I still cry for him sometimes at night, especially after I get one of his letters and I miss him all over again. If I do end up in the Pen, at least I'll get to see him.

I'm not sure what I'll do if I get out of subchapter 14. I guess I'll just keep running, moving from underground city to underground city, until things cool off and my parents and the authorities forget all about me. Then I'll try to make things right with the girl named Adele Rose.

My thoughts are running amok and I know it, but I can't seem to turn them off as I turn a corner, cutting a path through the back roads that will eventually get me to the heart of the city, where the train station lies. The strange route will add twenty minutes to my trip, but might protect me from the Enforcers.

In the darkness of a rarely travelled street, I feel somewhat safe, which is the first lesson I'll learn out on my own: you're never safe.

Feeling safe, I pass right by a stone stoop that sits just off the road at the front of a small house. There's a flash of red in my peripheral vision and I jerk my head to see what caused it. That's when I smell the bitter smoke from a freshly lit cigarette. My eyes zero in on the scene before me, taking in every awful detail before my brain can put it all together. Two men, both smoking, gazing off to the side, away from me, smoke curling around their heads. One of them is an Enforcer, dressed in bright sun dweller red, a gun and a sword hanging awkwardly from his belt as he sits on the steps, one knee raised higher than the other. An open door revealed the soft glow of candlelight.

Engrossed in their own thoughts, they haven't seen me yet, staring absently out onto the small front patio.

You're never safe.

But I do have half a chance because they're oblivious to my presence. My heart pounding in my chest, I back away slowly, retracing my steps in reverse, holding my breath as I move further and further from their field of vision.

Three steps from safety.

The non-Enforcer—a moon dweller who likely owns the house and trades cigarettes to the Enforcer in exchange for freedom from persecution—can no longer see me, as I move behind a wall.

Two steps.

The angle of the wall is such that I can still see the Enforcer, the crimson of his uniform like a warning beacon on the edge of my vision.

One step.

As if some inner instinct alerts him to my presence, his head snaps to the side and his black eyes lock on mine. He smiles.

I run.

Although I can't see him, my ears pick up the scuff and scrape of his shoes on stone as he moves off the stoop. He's not wasting any time coming after me, probably already feeling the excitement of the chase that will add some fun to his boring night. Maybe a juvenile girl breaking curfew is about the most excitement he ever gets, who knows? My only chance: get out of sight as quickly as possible. I might not be a fighter, but I am a runner.

I hear a shout as I cut a hard right down an alleyway. It's the obvious move, but the only one available. Lengthening my already-long strides, I abandon my quiet footsteps and thunder down the narrow path between the houses. The alley is longer than I'd like, and I know the Enforcer will enter it before I get to the end.

Get out of sight.

I listen to my own advice and swerve to the left, using a hand on the top of a chain-link fence to propel myself over it. Landing in a crouch on the other side, I make for a gap between the houses, cringing as I hear the rattling of the metal fence in my wake. I feel a sting of pain and warmth on my hand from the sharp barbs at the top of the fence, but I bite it back and dash to the front of the house.

I don't have time to open the front gate so I hurdle that, too, stumbling when I land awkwardly on the street. *Keep moving*, I urge myself, using my uninjured hand to catch my balance. From the property I just exited, I hear another shout, this one closer. Despite my efforts, the Enforcer is catching up.

Doing my best to ignore a twinge of pain in my ankle and the burning in my hand, I sprint down the road, running faster than I ever have before, my breathing ragged and gasping, my heart like a jackhammer in my chest. Up ahead there's an alley on the right and one on the left. Although it shouldn't be, it feels like a crucial decision. Right or left. Freedom or capture. Neither feels right as I approach the intersection, but I lean toward the left and prepare to dive in that direction, hopefully before the Enforcer gets out onto the road.

Just as I bend my knees and start to push off with my feet, I feel a rough hand grab a handful of my tunic and yank me hard to the right. Unless the Enforcer has been blessed with inhuman speed, it cannot be him; more likely it's another Enforcer that I didn't see or that was radioed in by his buddy. Either way, I'm toast.

And then I'm in the alley to the right, a firm hand over my mouth, kicking and clawing and bucking like a wild animal, desperately trying to get loose. A harsh voice hisses in my ear. "Quit yer fightin' or that Enfo will catch the both of us!"

I have no reason to obey the voice, but instinctively I do. I guess I've just always been a rule follower, not one to disobey an order. The second I calm down, the hand moves away from my lips and clamps around my arm, urgently pulling me further into the alley and behind a dumpster. I try to get a look at my captor (hero?) but all I get is a flash of thick, long dark hair attached to a sturdy frame. He's dressed in all black, nearly invisible even to my used-to-the-dark eyes.

He turns to face me and I catch a glimpse of a very young-looking face, before he whispers, "Under here," and throws a thick blanket over the both of us, casting us into darkness. "Get down," he commands.

I'm not sure how a blanket will protect us, but I have no choice but to trust this young stranger, who seems just as intent on avoiding detection by the Enforcer. I sprawl out on the rock alleyway, unconcerned with getting scraped and dirty. The guy with the young face is closer to me than I've ever been to a boy, and instantly I feel warm—hot even. The heat might have been slightly pleasant, if not for the putrid odor of rotting garbage that assaults my nostrils.

But now is not the time to complain, so I do my best to breathe through my nose and remain perfectly still. We're in place not a moment too soon, as we hear the pound of boots on rock, a pause, and then urgent footfalls heading right for us.

They get closer and closer until I swear he's about to step on us, and then stops with a suddenness that throws my heart into a frenzy. There's heavy breathing and a grumbling voice. "If I find you, you freaking little blond-haired bitch, we'll have a little fun before I turn you in, you mark my words. Damn strays, always making things harder than they have to be." There's a clang that almost makes me jump out of my skin as the Enforcer opens the dumpster lid. He's literally right next to us, searching through the garbage in case we're hiding inside. But why doesn't he see the blanket with the two human lumps under it?

After a few minutes of rummaging in the garbage, the lid slams shut with a frustrated *bang!* and the guy mumbles, "…might just have to kill you for putting me through all this trouble…" before scuffing away, his footsteps becoming more and more distant until they disappear into the night altogether.

Neither of us move or speak for what feels like hours, our bodies close and warm and covered in a haze of nose-plugging odor.

Finally, he speaks, his voice a low rumble under the blanket. "You okay?"

It feels like such a strange question after the rough way he manhandled me to safety. And yet, I sense he's not just being polite, but genuinely wants to know that I'm uninjured. "I think so," I say, flexing my sore ankle to check for a sprain. It's twisted, but not sprained. Definitely walkable. "I need to get going," I add.

"That guy will be back with more Enfos," he says. "We need a better place to hide."

"Better than a blanket?" I say, not meaning to make a joke, but unable to stop my mouth.

He laughs softly, which sounds even stranger under the circumstances. "It's a special blanket," he explains, which doesn't explain anything.

He stands up, simultaneously lifting the blanket off of me. The relatively fresh air hits my sweaty skin, immediately cooling it and raising goose bumps. "Here," he says, offering a hand.

I'm not one to deny a gentleman his small pleasures, so I take it, allowing him to pull me to my feet. It's probably just my imagination, but his fingers seem to linger on mine for a split-second longer than is necessary. Ever so slightly, the world lightens, as dawn begins when the panel lights on the cavern roofs switch on. With the added light, I see his face for the first time. He *is* young, perhaps my age, perhaps a year or two older. He's also indisputably handsome, with a strong jawline made rugged by the dark stubble of a three-day-old beard, dark brown eyes, and full, pink lips that appear to smile even when I know they're not. When he tosses the blanket in a pile next to the dumpster, I realize why the Enforcer missed us. The blanket is covered in garbage, to the point where you can't even see the fabric. With us under it, it would have just looked like a slightly bigger pile of trash, nothing worth investigating.

"Very clever," I say.

"They only ever check the dumpsters," the guy says. "They've got a lot of firepower, but they're not too bright."

"I take it you've done this before?"

He smiles, flashing a set of nice teeth. "You could say that. Let's go inside."

"The door will be locked," I say, pulling on the handle of a rusty metal door. As expected, it doesn't budge. "See."

"Don't tell me something as small as a locked door will stop a girl as motivated as you," he says, laughing at me with his deep, brown eyes.

I shrug, not knowing what to say. I'm too embarrassed to tell him I've never done *any* of this before.

"Don't worry, I could tell you were a *caker* from a mile away," he says.

I frown. "*Caker?*" I say, confused.

"Rich kid. Family with money. Cake eater."

Uh oh. This is the moment that always occurs when I try to make friends. It's happened to me my whole life. I meet new kids, try to be nice to people, but eventually they find out I belong to one of the few wealthy moon dweller families, and then—

—they hate me.

Except for Cole. He was never one to act like the other kids. But now, my short acquaintance with this guy is over, because he guessed where I come from. We didn't even get to the stage where we exchange names. He might even turn me in to the Enfo.

"I'm Roan," he says.

Huh? I just stare at him, waiting for the punch line, waiting for him to spit in my face, maybe even throw stones at me, like kids used to do before Cole put an end to all that.

He stares back, a goofy smirk resting easily on his face. "This is usually the point where you tell me your name, but if you don't want to…"

"My name?"

"Yeah, you know, like what your mother hollered out when the doc smacked you on the butt after you were born. Or did you want me to guess it?" Before I have a chance to say anything, he continues on, as if we're not hiding from the Enforcers in a deserted alleyway. "Hmm, I'd say you're a Violet. No wait, that's not it. You're Trudy, right?"

Is this guy serious? "Umm, Tawni."

"That was my next guess," he says. "So, *Tawni*, you coming in, or what?"

I gaze down the alley, expecting to see flashes of red as Enforcer reinforcements charge around the bend. But all I see is gray. Hiding out for a few minutes might not be a bad idea. "I've only got fifteen minutes," I say.

"Just enough time for breakfast," he says, sticking a hand in his pocket and pulling out a thin metal stick. "Step aside and make sure you're wearing your safety glasses—this might get messy."

Not having a clue what he's talking about, I move away from the door. With a couple of deft and experienced twists and turns of his wrist, he jams the stick—which I now realize is a pick—into the door's lock. I hear a clatter and a click and then the door opens, creaking slightly.

I just gawk at the door. "That was…" I murmur.

"Awesome, amazing, fan-freaking-tastic? Any of those will do, take your pick. Get it—*pick*," he says, holding up the metal wand.

I nod excitedly. "All of those things. It was really impressive. But is it legal?"

"Is whatever you're doing legal?" he retorts.

Even though I already know I'll have to break a number of rules along the way, his question still stings. Breaking the law doesn't come easily to me. "Fair enough," I say.

"After you," he says with a sweep of his hand. His second gentlemanly act.

I enter first, instinctively flicking on my flashlight amidst the inky darkness. The beam doesn't cut very far through the murk, but provides enough light to illuminate a concrete stairway immediately inside.

"Not much to look at, is it?" Roan says, stepping inside and easing the door shut. He reengages the lock by twisting a latch. "But it's still home."

"Your family lives here?" I ask incredulously.

"My *family* sold out to the Enfos a long time ago. I didn't stay with them after that. They never really liked me anyway."

I turn and take in Roan's shadow-darkened face, searching for a lie. There's none to be found. "I'm sorry," I say. "I'm leaving my family, too."

"Follow me," Roan says, barely brushing against me as he slips by and begins climbing the steps.

When we get to the top, he reaches back and grasps my hand, tugging me gently into a mostly-bare room off to one side. A thin bed pad and lantern sit on the dusty stone floor against one of the cracked walls. The stones, while mostly gray, have a greenish tint that looks anything but natural. The air smells musty and old and faintly of stale cigarettes. Releasing my hand, he says, "This is it. Home, sweet home."

I'm shocked. I've seen plenty of poverty in the Moon Realm, but this is beyond poverty. Roan has nothing. He should hate me for all that I have, but he doesn't seem to. Unless he's been biding his time, acting nice to get me inside, where no one would ever hear me cry out—

"I'm not going to hurt you," he says, an eyebrow raised.

Did he just read my mind? "How did you—"

"You look like someone just punched you in the gut. I know what you're thinking, and you're right not to trust people…like me. But I'm not like that. I just wanted to help you escape, to talk to you. I don't get the chance to make a lot of friends."

Oh. I feel rotten for having the thoughts I did. I can understand why Roan would be lonely in this place. It almost feels like a prison, only without bars on the windows and doors.

I want to change the subject. "Hey, can you teach me that lock-picking trick?"

His eyes light up. I've hit a happy topic. "Sure! It'll come in handy on the streets."

The streets. The phrase sounds so ugly, because…well, because it's true. The streets are my home now. I shrug it off. "Great," I say, trying to sound excited.

Grabbing my hand again, he pulls me outside the room and closes the door behind him. Looking so seriously into my eyes that it makes me blink faster, he says, "See, most locks have metal pins inside, the trick is to get them to all line up, as if there's a key in there…"

For the next twenty minutes—or is it an hour?—he teaches me, showing me sometimes, holding my hand to help me other times, and finally, letting me practice on my own. Just when I think I'll never get it, the lock clicks open!

"I did it!" I exclaim.

"Well done," he says. "You're a good student."

"You're a great teacher," I reply.

There's an awkward silence when he ducks his head sheepishly, as if not accustomed to being complimented.

"Well, I..." I start to say.

"Do you want some breakfast?" he asks suddenly.

"I should really be going..." I say.

"Another time then," he says, "do you know where you're going to live?"

"I have to leave subchapter 14," I say, realizing too late how stupid it is to share my plans with anyone else.

"Leaving? But why?"

"It's a long story," I say, not wanting to reveal any more than I have to. "I need to catch a train."

His dark eyes slowly brighten as he cocks his head to the side into the beam of his flashlight. After a few seconds chewing on his lip, he nods, as if he's made up his mind about something. "I'll take you to the station," he says. "You know, for safety," he adds.

"You really don't have to..."

"I *want* to," Roan says, shrugging.

Well, if he wants to... "Sounds great."

Although I've lingered far too long at Roan's place, we make up a lot of time on the way to the train station. Roan takes me on a crazy and convoluted route that I could never repeat on my own. Although we get within eyeshot of Enforcers several times, we never get close enough to feel threatened. By Roan's side, I feel safer than I thought I could possibly feel away from home. Even though I don't really know him, I feel like I trust him. If he wanted to hurt me, he already could have. It feels good being with someone, and I'm dreading reaching our destination. It's weird: I'm actually sort of enjoying running away while I'm with him.

But all good things have to come to an end.

Standing on crumbles of broken glass, we can see the entrance to the train station from our vantage point at the end of a shadowy alley. I've missed the beginning portion of the morning rush from our subchapter, but there are still plenty of late arrivers to keep things busy and hectic, which is exactly what I need.

Here goes nothing.

"Thank you, Roan," I say, meaning it. His kindness was an unexpected—and life-saving—part of my journey to this point.

He shrugs as if it's the kind of thing he does every day. "Sure. So there's nothing I can do to change your mind about going?" The smile that accompanies his words generates a burst of heat on my cheeks. I certainly wouldn't mind looking at his face a little while longer, but I've already delayed this too long and I'm afraid if I don't take the first step now, I never will.

"This is something I have to do," I say, trying to make my voice as deep and bold-sounding as I can.

He nods, like he already guessed my response. "Be careful, Tawni. If I'm lucky we'll meet again."

"I hope we do," I say, wishing I could drag the moment out a little longer. I've never liked goodbyes, even ones from people I don't know very well—or in this case, at all. But I manage to square my shoulders, face the train station, and find a tiny splinter of courage somewhere in my bones. I'm doing this to atone for the sins of my parents. If I can find Adele Rose, I'll tell her the truth about what they did to her family, and I'll do everything in my power to make things right.

My legs are suddenly like lead, but even that can't stop me. I lift one foot and force it forward, following it with the other foot. With each step I feel lighter, as if bits and pieces of a heavy burden are crumbling down from my shoulders. I feel alive.

I slink into a stream of adults making their way to the train station. Keeping my eyes straight ahead, I avoid looking at them for fear that "Alert! Delinquent!" might be written all over my face. But no one seems interested in me. They all have their own problems, which they face by trudging to the train every day, zombie-like expressions on their blank faces, hoping that they'll earn enough today to feed their families. Yeah, they've got bigger concerns than a sixteen-year-old girl who should be getting ready for school.

And then I'm inside the train station, so quickly that it almost feels like I blinked out of existence and back into it, not even passing through the arched entrance. I nearly forget to prepare my ticket and travel pass until I notice a woman who's scrambling for hers. Swinging my pack around, I locate the ticket and forged intra-Realm travel authorization card under a sachet of rice.

The automated turnstiles loom ahead, spinning as each rider scans their ticket and, depending on where they're going, their travel authorization. I've never ridden a train before, never left my subchapter, so I watch each traveler, memorizing the order of things. Ticket first, then pass, green light, push through the gate. Not so hard.

There are only five people in front of me, no more than ten seconds. The moment of truth. Will there be flashing lights and blaring alarms? Or will the green light blink, beckoning me through to a new life?

Four people. No wait, three people—two passed through while I was worrying.

Green light. Two people.

I realize I'm sweating profusely from my forehead. Make that my armpits. And kneepits, if there is such a thing. Everywhere, really. I'm a sweaty mess.

Green light. One person—the woman who was as unprepared as I, who now has her ticket ready, just like me.

My heart's pounding, both in my chest and my head. My knees feel rubbery, as if my bones have melted under me, congealing into a moldable substance that wobbles and totters like a two-year-old who still can't walk properly.

Green light. The woman passes through the turnstiles and for a moment the metal rungs look like scythes, cutting her to ribbons, severing her limbs like scissors against the arms of paper cutout dolls. I blink away the thought.

My turn.

I just stare at the ticket scanner, wondering what fate it holds for me. My mind goes blank. What goes first again? Pass or ticket? I know the answer should be obvious, but I just can't seem to remember. My mind is more muddled than bean stew.

"Move it," a gruff voice says from behind me.

If I don't hurry I'm going to draw a lot more attention to myself than I want. Ticket first, I remember. I scan my ticket, which I already know is valid. A dull beep sounds and a robotic voice says, "Please scan your travel authorization now."

I'm dead. I know it. I should just turn and leave now, before it's too late. Forget the strange and annoyed stares I'll get from the other passengers. Forget the shame I'll feel inside for having chickened out. Go back to Roan's place and let him teach me the ways of the street.

"Hurry up, kid!" A different voice this time, angrier than the first, and identifying me as a "kid," which is exactly the sort of tag I don't want. The instinct to run grows stronger and I start to turn, but then something pops into my head that stops me.

A face from the news. I watched it with my parents on the telebox, knowing full well it was them that had created this news story. The face of a young girl—my age. Adele Rose. Black, obsidian hair. Pale skin, like mine. Fierce, emerald-green eyes. Full lips. Pretty. A look on her face that could only be described as ugly. It was a face that told a tale of betrayal, of having her parents sold to the world as traitors, of being ripped from her family and sent to the Pen until she turns eighteen, and then to an adult prison, the Max, until the day she dies. All because of the actions of my parents. Not me—my parents. And yet I feel responsible.

The memory of her face stops me. Only I can turn her expression pretty again.

I turn and scan my fake travel pass, ready to be arrested if that is my fate.

The light turns green.

I can't help the smile that lights up my face as I stride forward, placing my hands on the push bar, which is cold and hard, but with rounded edges, not like the razor-sharp blade of a scythe at all. I did it—I'm leaving the subchapter at long last! I'm so full of elation that I literally feel bubbles of air rising in my chest, lifting my posture higher, buoying my spirits. I start to push the bar forward.

"Wait just a minute, kid!" I hear from behind.

When I turn I see red: a uniform, clean and bright; an Enforcer, his Taser raised, aimed directly at my chest; his face, a duplicate of the man I saw smoking a cigarette on a moon dweller stoop earlier this very morning.

"I told you I'd catch you," he snarls, pressing a button on his Taser.

Just before the snake of electricity pulls me into unconsciousness, I think, *I'm coming, Cole.*

AN ANTHOLOGY

Deeper- Two Tales from the Tri-Realms

David Estes

Before the creation of the Tri-Realms, and before there were moon dwellers, the inhabitants of the earth lived in relative safety. But then a massive meteor locked on a collision course with our planet. U.S. scientists had predicted it for years, using a substantial government-funded budget to carry out their contingency plan—a series of extraordinary caves and tunnels deep below the surface of the earth. Despite their efforts, however, when the harbinger of Armageddon arrived, there wasn't enough room for every U.S. citizen. Not nearly enough, in fact. A mere one percent of the population would be able to enter the hidden sanctuaries and start a new life. Who would be chosen? Who would be left to die above? No one could predict the outcome of The Lottery.

*To my beautiful wife, Adele, without whom
I would be lost.*

AN ANTHOLOGY

The Life Lottery – A Story from Year Zero

Today is The Lottery. It's been the only thing anyone's talked about for the last week.

My mom said it would never happen, that the government would come to their senses, come up with a new plan. My dad said the whole world's gone crazy. Now that the day is here, it looks like my dad was right.

The guy on the news says that the countries aren't speaking to each other anymore, that it's every country for itself. That just seems sad to me. I once had a pen pal named Sophia from France. I worry about her. I wonder if France has a Lottery too.

The Lottery in the U.S. is "a bag of baloney," my dad says. By that I think he just means it's not a good system. I pretty much agree with him, because I don't want to be split up with my family. The way it works is that every person of every age has the same chance of getting picked. The government says that's the only way it can be equal, because if they did it by family, the smaller families would have an equal chance of being selected as a larger family, and it might mess up the number of people who are allowed to go underground. Only three million can fit in the caves, they say. No exceptions! I can still see the President's finger pointing at the camera, as if he's yelling at me personally.

I might be only twelve years old, but even I don't think it feels like the right rules. I mean, what if my dad gets picked and not my mom? Or my sister, Tina, and not me? Or what if everyone *except* me gets picked? What would I do then? Who will I live with until the meteor comes?

But there's no arguing with the government people. Once they decide something, that's it. End of story. Only for the rest of us, it's not the end of the story—it's only the beginning.

My mom gave me this diary this morning so I could "share my experiences and pass them down to my children." I think she's being rather optimistic, but I didn't tell her that. I'm scared I'm not doing a very good job with it so far; I mean, I haven't even told you my name. Anna Lucinda Smith. There—I guess that covers that.

At school I have lots of friends, but it's not like I'm stuck up about it or anything. I just get along with most people, I guess. Not that we have school anymore. Ever since the announcement, pretty much everything's been cancelled. My parents won't even let me go outside, because everyone's going crazy and breaking into stores and stealing stuff and all that nonsense. I've seen all that on the news, but not in person. My neighborhood has mostly been quiet, with people just staying inside, spending time with their families. It would actually be kind of cool getting out of school for a few days if it weren't for the whole world-ending thing.

It's been a little boring, too, so I started playing this game I made up. I cut up a hundred strips of paper. On four of them I wrote "Anna", "Tina", "Mom" and "Dad". Then I put them in a bowl and mixed them all around. With my eyes closed, I take turns picking out a name. After reading it and marking it on a score sheet, I stick the name back in the bowl and try again. Most of the time I just get a blank piece of paper, which means some random stranger was selected to go underground. But every once in a while I get a hit. So far I've picked random strangers eighty six times, my mom twice (she's always been the lucky one in the family), my dad once—and even I got picked once. Only Tina hasn't come up yet, but I think that's because she'll be the one to get chosen in the real Lottery. Anyway, the game passes the time.

My parents are out for some registration thing they had to do in advance of The Lottery tonight, and my sister is in her room listening to her iPod and obsessing over some guy that she hopes will get chosen with her. She thinks it would be so romantic to go underground with this guy, like something out of a movie. Although I've seen the guy, and he *is* cute, this isn't a movie. In any case, I'm alone again so I play my game for another two hours. I pick out one hundred and thirty three strips of paper.

None of them have a name on it.

Not a good sign for tonight.

I'm thankful when my parents get home because I'm feeling depressed about the game. I don't tell my mom though because she's been telling me all week not to play it.

Mom makes lunch—salami and provolone cheese, my favorite!—while Dad scoops ice cream into tall glasses and pours Root beer on top. All the while they keep up a constant chatter about how nice and sunny it is outside—cold, but nice—how we should all go in the backyard and spend time together later, and how beautiful the leaves are now that they're changing. I've never heard them so cheery, which scares me.

After lunch, the day whizzes by, like it's sprouted wings and flown south for the winter. Tina refuses to come out of her room. I don't feel like going outside either, but I finally give in to my parents and follow them to the backyard. We sit cross-legged in the grass for a while, which feels weird and awkward, probably because it's something we've never done before—I mean, why would we?

Dad has a ball, which we pass around. Each time someone catches it, they have to say something that they love about the person who threw it to them. Although I know what Tina would call the game—"Totally cheese ball!"—I kind of like it. Not only do my parents say some really nice things about me—my dad says I'm "as pretty as a flower," and my mom says my sense of humor "is as good as your father's," which is saying something, because Dad's pretty funny—but I also get to hear them say some nice things to each other. I'm not embarrassed to admit that I'm disappointed when the game ends and we go inside to eat dinner.

Tina finally makes an appearance, although she doesn't talk much, just types out "later texts" on her phone, which I guess are texts she'll send to Brady—her guy—after The Lottery is over. She says they're all positive messages which will help their karma, so they both get picked. I don't ask her what messages she's sending for me so I'll get picked. I also don't tell her that she never gets chosen in my game.

Dinner is delicious: my mom's famous meatloaf and creamy mashed potatoes, drowned in brown gravy. Hot fudge sundaes for dessert this time, compliments of Dad.

When we finish, we get dressed in nice clothes, as if we're going to church. Dad says there will be lots of photographers at each of the local Lotteries, taking pictures for future history books. I wear a medium-length purple dress with amethyst beading that Tina once admitted makes me look "all grown up." When we meet downstairs she gives me a nod as if to say, "Nice choice," which makes me smile. She, on the other hand, tries to slip past Dad in a tiny black skirt and a tight, low-cut red blouse. He makes her change twice before she finally gets it right. I guess even on Lottery Day, he's still a dad.

Dad wears his best suit and a pink tie that almost makes him look like another person. Mom is in her favorite blue gown—the one with all the sparkles.

Like everyone else, we walk to the school, where The Lottery will be held. It's slow going, because Tina and Mom are wearing heels, clopping along with short strides. I'm glad I wore my ballet flats.

Dozens of other families are doing the same, and we greet many of them with cheerful cries of "Hello!" and "How are you?" They answer with the same forced cheerfulness.

We arrive at the school and enter the auditorium through the propped-open double doors. Dad hands some papers to man at a desk who then signals us forward. Already the hall is half full. Ushers direct us up one of the aisles and into the next available row. Normally I'd want to sit by one of my friends, Maddy or Bridget or Haley, who I spot sitting a few rows forward, but I know tonight is meant to be spent with family. Even Tina sits with us, which she never does these days.

Despite all the greetings and warm wishes that were exchanged outside of the auditorium doors, once inside, no one speaks to each other, or even smiles. It's like we all know that the others are our enemies, people who will strip us of our winning ticket in The Lottery, take away our family and friends.

Not long after we arrive, the auditorium fills up. I stare at the empty stage, where I once stood dressed like a tree in the school play, *The Wizard of Oz*. Now it looks barren and desolate, like a hot, dusty stretch of desert. Mom checks her watch and shows it to me: one minute until eight o'clock. Time for The Lottery.

She squeezes my hand and holds on.

All is silent in the hall, not even a whispered comment breaking the quiet. Footsteps echo onto the stage as a man who I recognize from TV moves across to a podium in the center. A local politician. The mayor or governor or something like that. The man in charge tonight.

When he reaches the stand, the microphone cuts his face in half, so he lowers it until it's even with his lips. He speaks, his voice magnified and deep, like the real Wizard of Oz from the movie.

"Residents of the Sawcutter School District of the great state of Pennsylvania. Today is a momentous occasion in the history of our great country." Although he looks up every couple of words, his voice sounds stiff, scripted, like he's reading off of something, perhaps a hidden paper on the podium. "I know you all must be scared, because you have little control over the random selection that is about to be made, but remember that this is an opportunity to defeat the cosmic powers that strive to wipe us off the face of the earth. For the first time in history, a species has had the wherewithal and foresight to prepare for just such an event. We will not be forced into extinction! We will fight to survive, whether above or underground! We cannot be defeated!"

He spouts the last three sentences with such conviction that it's like he's leading a pep rally, trying to get us all pumped up for The Lottery, but his words fall flat on our ears and we just stare at him. Mom glances at Dad and he rolls his eyes.

"Well, uh, I guess we should get started then," the guy says when no one applauds. "First, the formalities. The names of all five thousand, two hundred and forty six residents of this district have been entered into a database, sorted alphabetically by last name. When I press a button, the computer will randomly select a name from the database, simultaneously removing it from the list. I will read out the name. I ask that you try to keep your celebrating to a minimum so that I can move on to the next name. As announced by the President of the United States a week ago today, each citizen of this country will receive a one in one hundred chance of being chosen, and therefore, I will read out fifty two names for this district. Good luck."

He pauses and I remember my game, remember how excited I got when I opened my eyes to see that I'd picked one of my family members. If I magnify that feeling by a million, that's how excited I know I'll be if all of us get picked today.

He reads the first name: "Helen Chambers."

Somewhere behind us a woman squeals in delight, but I don't look back. That name is foreign to me. I close my eyes, wait for the next name.

Another stranger—a blank strip of paper. No one worth getting excited over.

Ten more names—ten more strangers. I flinch with each one. And then—

Maddy gets picked! My eyes flash open and I look where I know she's sitting. She's smiling as her mother puts an arm around her shoulders, hugging her, but she also looks kind of scared and I know why: no one else in her family has been chosen.

More names, more exclamations of excitement, more blank names on white pieces of paper. Although I've tried to keep track, I've lost count of how many names have been called. One of my neighbors gets picked, a guy who's always been nice to me, bought Girl Scout Cookies from me and said hello when I walked by, but I realize I'm not happy for him…because he's not my family. Like the rest of the people around me, he's the competition.

Three, four, five, six names: not us. Enemies.

There's a pause and my breath catches in my throat. Is that it? Has The Lottery ended so quickly without warning? Will my family go home without a ticket, left to face the meteor with the rest of those not chosen?

"Ten spots left," the man says, and I let out my breath. A warning. A bone. A shred of hope. Almost like a redo, like in my game when I pick out a blank paper, I can just put it back and try again. Ten more tries.

"Morgan Rivers." A stranger in the front row.

"Willow Meadows." Sounds like a made up name.

"Robert Dorsett." Who?

Seven left.

Three no-names and then a man my father works with. Three left.

"Meghan Taurasi." Never heard of her.

"Brian Henderson." An older man two rows in front of us tips his brown bowler hat at the stage.

One left. He pauses, scans the audience, as if he's taking in each of the faces, knowing full well he has bad news for most of us. Ten seconds go by and I wonder if I miscounted, if Mr. Henderson was the last name the computer has for us.

But then he clears his throat and speaks: "Anna L. Smith."

AN ANTHOLOGY

About the Author

David Estes is the author of five YA novels and four children's books. He was born in El Paso, Texas but moved to Pittsburgh, Pennsylvania when he was very young. David grew up in Pittsburgh and then went to Penn State for college. Eventually he moved to Sydney, Australia where he met his wife. A reader all his life, he began writing novels for the children's and YA markets in 2010, and started writing full time in June 2012. Now he travels the world writing with his wife, Adele. David's a writer with OCD, a love of dancing and singing (but only when no one is looking or listening), a mad-skilled ping-pong player, and prefers writing at the swimming pool to writing at a table.

Buy *The Moon Dwellers* on Amazon, Barnes & Noble, and Smashwords.

 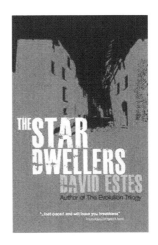

Learn more about David and his books at:

http://davidestesbooks.blogspot.com
Follow David on Twitter @Davidestesbooks
Like David at: http://www.facebook.com/Davidestesbooks
Add David on Goodreads at http://www.goodreads.com/davidestesbooks

AN ANTHOLOGY

Broken

As Part of The Syrenka Series

Amber Garr

Life as a mermaid can be suffocating.

Eviana and her friends live in a hidden world at the precipice of civil war. Their powers are new, their responsibilities daunting. Forced to decide the fate of their kind, a decision made in haste will have lasting repercussions. When Eviana chooses to run away from it all, she hurts those who love her most, especially her fiancé.

Ever wonder how Kain felt on their wedding day? Or how the return trip to California tested the bounds of Eviana's relationship with her friends? In *Cold Feet*, Kain witnesses Eviana's deceit and is forced to deal with the consequences of her behavior. In *Rift*, Daniel encourages the group to make a detour to the Grand Canyon, as the distance between the friends begins to rival the great ravine.

For Beth. I miss you every day.

AN ANTHOLOGY

Cold Feet

Eviana wrapped her arms around me as I spoke. "I'm going to go too. We have a big day tomorrow." I smiled, imagining how radiant she'd look. The scent of the bonfire still lingered in her hair and I rubbed her back wishing we could prolong this moment. Despite our kiss earlier in the day, I sensed she wasn't completely comfortable with the plans for tomorrow. Our wedding.

Deciding to give her some space, I stepped back and gently moved her hands away. "I will see you in the morning, Eviana. Sleep well." Without a second thought, I bent forward and kissed her. Just a slight brush against the lips, it wasn't as intense as the first one, but enough to let her know I cared.

I walked out the door and toward my car, knowing I should listen to that nagging feeling in the pit of my stomach. *She's just nervous*, I thought as I rehashed our earlier conversation on the beach.

"You're a good man, Kain," she'd said. "Please know that. And if something were to happen to me, I want you to find someone else and be happy with them. Don't mourn me. Don't hate me. Just live your life."

I couldn't understand what she meant. "Why would I hate you?"

She squeezed my hands as tears leaked down her cheeks. "Just promise me that you will live and move on. Please!"

Her behavior had worried me, so I kissed her forehead. "Okay, I promise. Now stop crying," I teased, trying to lighten the situation. How could I ever hate her?

Backing out of the driveway now, my thoughts spiraled out of control. There could only be one reason why she would worry about me hating her, but I didn't think Eviana would skip out on our wedding. Not after today. Not after she stood by my side at my father's memorial and my appointment ceremony as my fiancée, and especially not after our first kiss. She cared about me, I knew it. It might not be in the same way she loved the selkie, but she would come around.

She had to.

By the time I pulled into the hotel parking lot, I realized sleep wasn't going to happen. The clan shield on my shirt vibrated with power and a ball of dread rumbled in my stomach. If Eviana was having second thoughts, I needed to be there for her. Why did I leave?

I turned the car around and headed back toward her beach house. The dark night swallowed my headlights, creating an ominous void. Call it intuition or just a hunch, something felt wrong the moment before I rounded the curve that hid her driveway.

Brendan's car sat at the end of the lane, engine idling for a quick escape. My heart dropped as angry blood filled the void. She wouldn't do this.

I pulled off the side of the road, far enough away to avoid detection, but close enough to watch the events unfold. Deciding to torture myself even more, I felt my body leave the car behind and walk closer to hear the exchange. In a haze of resentment and disappointment, I crept along the side of the road, hidden amongst the shrubbery. The sharp leaves and branches lashed at my face but were nothing more than a minor discomfort in comparison to my frantic heart.

I stopped when Brendan opened the door and walked around the front of the car. His smile confirmed my worst fear, and it took all of my self control not to jump up and knock it off his face. For the life of me, I didn't understand why she always chose that selkie. I also didn't know why I tortured myself thinking that things would turn out any differently.

I heard the grinding of her suitcase being dragged across the ground before I saw her. Panic, rage, and sadness washed over me with such intensity I almost lost my balance. Should I stop her? Should I give her one last chance to do what was right? We needed this marriage to unite our clans at a time when politics were unstable and volatile. And I needed this marriage because I loved her. However, that realization crawled back into the depths of my consciousness when I saw them kiss.

"You made it," Brendan said.

"Of course I did. I wouldn't miss this for the world." Eviana reached up to kiss him again, and something inside of me changed. She never looked at me that way, in fact I never saw her as happy as she was right now, in the midst of running away from everything she knew.

Brendan grabbed her suitcase and she slipped into the car. A few moments later they pulled away from the driveway and headed in the opposite direction. I watched as the taillights disappeared, unable to move. Was it disbelief? Was it anger? Eviana chose Brendan instead of her family, her clan, and me. It was selfish and childish, but for some reason, I couldn't fault her. If I could have run away from my life, I probably would have done the same.

Thinking about it some more, I wondered what my father would have thought if I'd refused to accept clan leadership. It would have crushed him and my mother. We can't choose the families we are born into, and Eviana should understand that better than anyone.

But can we choose whom to love? I've been in love with Eviana since we were kids, knowing that I would do anything for her. As we got older, those feelings intensified when I watched her coach the young merfolk through their first transitions. Or when I'd see the feistiness I knew would benefit her as a leader someday. I loved her just as much as she loved Brendan.

Suddenly I got it. If Eviana asked me to run away with her, I would have done it in a second. Knowing that would've never happened, I still understood what they must have felt when she and Brendan decided this was their only choice. I'd given her another option; marry me and continue her relationship with Brendan. We would have ruled together as expected, and I would still have some part of her by my side. But even as I said those words to her weeks ago, I'd secretly hoped she wouldn't take me up on my offer. I wouldn't have been able to bear it.

A noise in the distance startled me. Dragging my feet back to the car I fell inside and started the engine. The sun would be up in four hours, and I'd have to face the world knowing I was second choice.

Deciding to stay here until the morning, I parked in her family's driveway and walked past the house down to the beach. I needed the comfort of the water, although in too much of a daze to think about transitioning. Passing the smoldering bonfire from earlier tonight, anger seized control. I picked up an empty bottle and threw it against the logs, waiting for the sound of smashing glass to consume the night. How could she do this to me? The sand muffled my screams as I threw another and another, trying to cope. I hated her so much.

Moving closer to the water, I dropped to the ground. The ocean covered my legs like a blanket and I ignored the tingling that signaled the need to transform. Instead, I sat on the sand, listening to the surf, and compartmentalizing all of my emotions into their own little box. Disappointment, love, hate, and devastation each took their turn churning through my sea of denial.

For hours I sat there reminiscing about the past and figuring out the future. Would I ever see her again? Did I even want to? Her mother would be furious, as this was not only an embarrassment to the family but would reflect poorly on her leadership skills in the eyes of those who desired change. A lone gull laughed at me in the same way the other clan leaders would when they discovered tonight's events.

As soon as I saw the first glimmer of sunrise, I trudged back up to the house and tried to prepare myself for the humiliation to come. Though early morning, a flurry of movement reminded me that wedding preparations were in full swing. I sighed as I took that last, heavy step up to the expansive wood deck. No amount of preparation would make this any easier.

The sliding glass door slid open with a thud, and three protectors emerged carrying large vases of flowers. Troy saw me standing in the shadows and nodded in my direction.

"Master Matthew. I didn't know you were here already."

I tried to make my smile look authentic. "Couldn't sleep."

He set the heavy arrangement down and wiped a bead of sweat from his face. "Getting cold feet yet?" he teased.

My stomach flipped and I swallowed the anger in my throat. Instead of replying I forced out a laugh. This wouldn't be easy. I was here and no one knew Eviana was gone. *Who do I tell first?*

"Is Mistress Dumahl inside?" I asked, deciding on her mother, the leader of their clan.

"Yes, in the banquet room I believe," Troy said.

I nodded to him and walked inside the house. Moving around the center island, I couldn't help but notice the flowers and baskets and wedding decorations scattered all over the place. A lot had gone into the planning of this wedding, and a lot of people were going to be very disappointed.

As I rounded the corner, I ran into a petite woman carrying a clipboard and yelling into her cell phone.

"No, I said fuchsia, not pink. You better not show up here with pink bows." She looked up with a glare before recognizing me. "I'm not arguing about this anymore. Just be here soon." She hung up and shook her head. "I tell you, give someone a little leeway and they think they can redesign the whole wedding."

"Mistress Dumahl," I said. "I need to…"

"Please, call me Marguerite, Kain. You're a part of this family now." She beamed at me with a smile that perfectly matched Eviana's. I sucked in a breath. "I wasn't expecting you so early, but I'm glad you're here. Perhaps you can get her out of bed?"

"Eviana? But I need to talk to…"

"Yes," she said and brushed past me. "Please tell Eviana that I need her downstairs in twenty minutes."

Before she finished that sentence, her phone rang again. I heard her yelling at yet another vendor as she marched through the house. Tempted to leave, I stood there weighing the pros and cons of that decision. I could just slip away until they noticed Eviana had left and let them break the news to me. That would be easier, but that would also be cowardly.

I looked up toward the stairs thinking about climbing them. Maybe Eviana left a note. Maybe she had a good reason as to why she snuck out in the middle of the night to run away with her boyfriend. Maybe, but probably not.

I found myself walking up them anyway. A door at the top of the stairs opened and I almost ran into Eviana's sister. She rubbed her eyes and tugged on her pajama top before noticing my presence.

"Kain?" Marisol tried to smooth out her hair. She smiled and then quickly covered her mouth. I saw color rise to her cheeks. "What are you doing here so early?" She stepped back into her room.

"I couldn't sleep."

"Sorry, I just didn't know you would be here before I had a chance to get ready. I mean, Eviana."

Marisol always had a crush on me, and I felt a little less anxious as I watched her try to avoid blowing her morning breath in my direction. "Your mother wants me to wake her up." *Even though she isn't here.*

Marisol chuckled. "Good luck with that. She doesn't like getting up early."

I thanked her for the warning and walked to the end of the hall. This was it. Time to face the cold, hard truth. I knocked on the door before remembering it was unnecessary. Despite all of the commotion downstairs, the hallway remained empty and desolate. Just me and my fear of what I knew I would find inside filled the void.

Opening the door, I held my breath. My hands shook, my stomach turned, and I couldn't decipher whether it was anger or heartbreak that ripped apart my insides. A persistent sliver of light filtered in between the curtains, highlighting a single spot on Eviana's bed. As though there for a purpose, the beam shone directly on an envelope I knew would be addressed to me.

I swallowed my pride and the fear clawing at my throat, and walked to the bed to sit down next to her note. Sure enough, I saw my name. I only took a brief second before tearing it open, a glutton for punishment as always.

Kain-

These past few days with you have been enjoyable but confusing. I don't know if I will ever have the right words to explain why I left except to say this isn't the life I want.

My mother will be furious and my clan will be disappointed, but most of all, you will hate me. And that saddens me more than you'll ever know. There were many days when I wished I didn't have to choose. You are one of the most important people in my life, and I admit there were times when I wanted you to be enough. I'm sorry to leave like this, Kain. You deserve better.

Eviana

Reading over it three times, I finally let reality settle in. She was gone and not coming back. She left with Brendan and abandoned everyone who cared about her. A part of me wanted to mourn the loss, but the bitter and annoyed side won out. I wouldn't mourn for her. I felt too angry.

A shuffling at the door grabbed my attention. "Where is she?" Marisol asked.

I stayed seated on the bed, holding her note in my hand. Clearing my throat, I decided the time had come to let everyone know. "She's gone."

"What?"

I lifted my arm and shook the note. "She left with Brendan. Last night. She's not coming back." I struggled to get the words out.

Marisol stood in silence, mouth opened and sleepiness long gone from her eyes. Finally she spoke. "But she can't do that to you."

I laughed. It wasn't that I found Marisol's comment funny; it screamed irony. "Apparently she can," I replied and jumped to my feet. "I need to tell your mother." Pushing past Eviana's sister, I marched down the hall and toward the stairs with false bravado. Marguerite would not be pleased.

"Oh, she's going to be so mad," Marisol said. She scampered behind me, ready to see her mother's reaction. Marisol and Eviana did not get along well on most days, and this would surely be a memorable screw up for her big sister. Suddenly, Marisol tugged on my shoulder, forcing me to turn around and face her. Throwing her arms around my waist, she squeezed me hard. "I'm so sorry, Kain. She doesn't deserve someone like you."

A rush of dread skittered through my chest. Marisol was right, she didn't deserve me. "I know," I replied before continuing downstairs.

It proved easy to find Marguerite by the incessant yelling. I found her in the banquet room, directing the organization of the layout. It looked like the rental company brought the pink bows after all.

"Do you understand that this is my oldest daughter's wedding? It has to be perfect," she said to the poor man holding fifty pounds of chair covers. "Go find your boss." He slunk away while he had the chance, giving me the opening I needed.

"Marguerite, I have to talk to you."

"Kain, oh good. Did you get Eviana up?" She looked past me, but found only her youngest daughter staring back. The clan leader's eyes scrutinized the both of us, not missing anything. "What's going on?"

I pushed the paper into her hand. She looked at it, puzzled like she held a foreign object. Without saying another word, she opened the note. I watched as her face ran through a gauntlet of expressions from perplexed to stunned to furious in a matter of seconds.

"Is this some kind of joke?" At first I thought she'd spoken to me, but then noticed she directed the question to Marisol.

"Mom? No! I would never joke about such things." Marisol cowered behind me, trying to avoid the look that so many merfolk feared from their leader.

Marguerite glanced up at me one more time, and whatever she saw on my face must have convinced her of the truth. Her eyes glimmered with unshed tears. "Kain, I'm so sorry for the behavior of my child. I...," she cleared her throat, "I have to go take care of this."

For a brief moment, the Dumahl clan leader rested her tiny hand on my arm. Her disappointment mimicked my own, but now we had to clean up the mess. I wondered if Eviana thought about any of this before leaving.

"Marisol, come on. We need to find your father." The remaining Dumahl ladies left the room in search of answers they would never find. I needed to do something. And the first objective was to get out of this house.

Walking through the barrage of vendors and staff nearly sent me into a fit. I felt trapped. Constricted. When I finally pushed through the front doors, I could breathe again.

I climbed into my car without knowing where I wanted to go. *Just away from here*, I decided. Marguerite would call when she had a plan, which I knew would involve a clan punishment for Eviana if her mother's looks were any indication.

This problem belonged to Eviana now, and as I drove away from her home, I realized how much it was my problem too.

AN ANTHOLOGY

Rift

"Please, Kain. We need to get out of this car." Daniel squeezed his narrow shoulders between the two front seats and continued to beg. "I can't stand one more minute in this icy environment."

Kain rolled his head and gripped the steering wheel hard enough for me to see white knuckles. After driving a day and a half in tense silence, I agreed with Daniel. We all needed a break from each other.

"We don't have time," Kain replied.

"We have plenty of time," Daniel countered. "Are you really that anxious to get back home? I'm sure Eviana's not."

"Daniel!" I reached across the back seat and punched him in the shoulder.

"Ow, that hurt." He rubbed his arm and turned back to the front. "See, she's abusing me. We need a pit stop before this gets violent."

"And just where would you like to go?" Kain asked. I heard the defeat in his voice. Daniel had won, even if he didn't know it yet.

"Like I told you a million times, the Grand Canyon. We've seen the road signs for the last two hours. I've never been there and I'd hate to miss it when we're this close." Daniel patted Carissa's head while she sat motionless in the passenger seat. "Carissa wants to go there too."

She not so gently pushed his hand away and smoothed her hair. "I'd rather go home," she grumbled.

"What? You want to see one of the Wonders of the World?" Daniel asked. "Me too! See Kain, we all want to go."

Carissa turned to look out the window, making sure to avoid eye contact at all costs. She hadn't spoken much since she caught Kain and me in our almost kiss right before we started our trip. Despite having time together as we drove through the night, it looked like their issues remained unresolved. Apparently, she wasn't thrilled with Daniel either.

"Come on, Kain. It's early enough to get in a few hours," Daniel pleaded. "You can practice your compulsion skills and torment the humans. It'll be fun."

I enjoyed Daniel's charm, especially when he used it on someone else. For a few days, I never thought I'd get to see him again, let alone have his friendship. I saw a glimmer of amusement pass over Kain's face and knew he was contemplating that scenario. Sometimes using our powers helped direct the anger and frustration elsewhere.

And Kain felt frustrated. I knew him too well. The way he kept twisting his neck and the random sighs he'd let out, clued me in. I caught his eyes a few times in the rear view mirror, afraid of what I might see. He had every right to hate me, but I knew the frustration I saw came from the fact he didn't. Regardless of the mess I'd forced him to deal with when I left home, he still cared.

All three of my friends in this car cared. I'd been shunned, abjured from my clan, and yet they risked their lives to help me and my boyfriend, Brendan. A hole ripped open in my gut and daggers sliced apart my insides with that thought. Brendan. He left me. After everything we'd been through and everything I sacrificed for him, he feared me and my control over selkies. Discovering my ability to control him had been a surprise for me too. One that I hoped we could deal with together. But he freaked out, and was now on his way to Seattle to "take some time" and think about our relationship.

I didn't know if I should be angry or devastated. My emotions had run the gauntlet over the last several days, and now I felt numb. Perhaps utilizing my power over humans would help me out of this funk.

"Yes!" Daniel squealed.

I looked up to see Kain maneuvering the car into the exit lane announcing the route to the Grand Canyon. Smiling, I nestled back into my seat. A slap on my thigh pulled my attention to Daniel who waved colorful brochures back and forth in his hands.

"Here, take a look and see which part of the park we have time to see."

"Where did you get these?" I asked, amused with his preparedness.

"The truck stop. I told you, I've always wanted to go and I knew I could convince him." He beamed at me and slapped Kain on the shoulder. No one could stay mad at Daniel.

"We're only staying for two hours," Kain said.

"We'll see," Daniel mumbled, focused more on his brochure than Kain's demand.

"Two hours, Daniel. I want to get home tonight."

"Me too," Carissa added without looking at anyone.

"Okay, okay. Two hours. Geez." Daniel shook his head. "I feel like I'm trapped in a car with my parents."

I found it amusing to think about Kain and Carissa having a child like Daniel. But then my mood shifted. Even though I didn't deserve to think otherwise, I couldn't imagine Kain and Carissa having a future together. It was too painful, and someday I would need to address those feelings among many others.

"This is it!" Daniel shoved a cardboard brochure in my face.

I took one look and shook my head. "No way."

"What?"

"There is absolutely no way I am going out on that thing." The Skywalk was a four thousand foot high glass walkway jutting out over the canyon. Nothing but a few pieces of glass between the path and a very long fall. "Nope. No way, especially with all of those people on it."

"Oh, don't be a baby," Daniel teased. "You can use your powers to move them out of the way."

"Let me see," Carissa said, turning around and looking at me for the first time today. I smiled and passed her the pamphlet. She skimmed over the front and back and said, "I'll do it."

Of course she would.

"Sweet," Daniel said, snatching the brochure out of her hands. "Let's see...we can do the tour in two hours and still have time to hike around a bit."

"No, we have a long drive," Kain said, killing the mood.

"*No, we have a long drive,*" Daniel mocked in a ridiculous voice. "Fine. There's the exit."

Kain swerved rather quickly into the right lane, tossing Daniel back into his seat. Unfazed, he continued rambling about the history of the Skywalk and the Hualapai Indians. I listened for a while until my thoughts drifted back to the reality of my situation. Every time I envisioned going home, my stomach dropped in fear. Not only had I been shunned, but I was now the rightful leader of my clan. The family shield had chosen my destiny but I worried that my people wouldn't accept me. Especially my sister.

Thinking of Marisol crushed any excitement I may have had. She didn't know about my parents and I would have to break the news about their deaths. She'd hate me. She already hated me. I really didn't want to go home. Daniel had been right.

We arrived at the famous Skywalk an hour later. The parking lot looked relatively empty and devoid of any tour buses. We'd beat the crowd. Kain would be happy.

Daniel jumped out of the car before Kain turned off the ignition. His enthusiasm started to spread as the rest of us climbed out at a normal pace and took in our surroundings. The morning sun hadn't yet warmed the air, leaving it crisp and cool. Reds, oranges, and browns speckled the landscape like the kelp forests of California. My skin tingled with a familiar sensation when it recognized water nearby. It may have been thousands of feet below, but we were attuned to the element. I marveled at the massive canyon long enough to get a nudge.

"You coming?" Kain asked.

I looked up to see Daniel and Carissa walking toward the ticketing area. How long had I been standing there? "I can't go out on that."

Kain chuckled. "The heights?"

"Yes. And the glass floor. You know how I am on a plane." Kain had been instrumental in helping me cope with my fear of flying. I think it amused him more than anything.

"Maybe there's something else we can do," he said.

Stunned, I raised my eyebrows. I thought the last thing Kain would want is to spend any alone time with me.

He laughed again. "Don't look so surprised."

"You should experience the canyon," I said. "When are you ever going to be here again? It's not like we'll have much free time once we get home." My stomach cramped again and I shivered with dread.

Kain put his hands in his pockets and kicked a piece of gravel to the other side of the lot. "True."

Disappointed with his answer, I surprised myself when I said, "But I would love to have the company."

He looked down at me and smiled. "Maybe there's a trail we can hike while they try out the walkway."

Grateful, I squeezed his arm. "Thanks."

We almost made it to the walkway entrance when Daniel and Carissa bounded over to us. Daniel definitely had more spring in his step, but Carissa at least cracked a smile.

"You better hurry up and get your tickets. They only let small groups of people walk on it at a time," Daniel said.

"We're going to hang out around here," Kain said, cautious with his words.

Carissa bit her lip and stopped moving. She stared at Kain with an intensity I would have cowered under. But he held his ground, and after a brief standoff, continued the discussion.

"Eviana and I have a few things to discuss before we get back to California. Go on, you two enjoy the tour. We'll be right over there." Kain nodded toward a sign with a stick figure hiker and tent symbol.

"Can't you take a quick break from clan politics?" Daniel asked, his tone full of disappointment. Carissa remained silent.

"No, he's right. I need to know what I'm walking into," I said. "Besides, you couldn't force me on that thing." I smiled at Carissa, trying to make light of the situation, but she remained cold. A part of me wanted to convince her I wasn't after Kain. My broken heart belonged to someone else. But the other part of me decided to stay quiet.

"Well, you two suck and you're going to miss out." Daniel draped his arm over Carissa's shoulders; an awkward move considering her model height. "See you in three hours," he called out, kicking up dust in his wake.

"Two hours," Kain reminded him.

I chuckled. "He'll keep pushing."

"I know." Kain sighed. "We really do need to catch up on a few things."

More than a few, I thought to myself. The tension between us had never been so severe. At least when he first came to the east coast to help me, he had been angry. I knew my boundaries then. But ever since the brief moment before our departure, when we almost kissed, I didn't know where things stood. If there was one person in this world who could understand what I was going through now, it was Kain. However, I feared I'd lost him as a friend forever.

Swallowing the lump in my throat, I shuffled along his side to the trail entrance. A family with six kids pulled up next to us, annoying me with their energy. Kids screamed, parents yelled, and the serenity of the landscape dissipated. My head hurt as I struggled with my conscience- do I control them or not?

Kain noticed my focus and placed his hand on my lower back, guiding us away from the circus. "Don't do it," he said.

"I wasn't going to," I lied.

He smiled and my heart melted. One look like that and I second guessed every decision I made. Kain would have been good to me, but I ruined it for everyone. He needed me to stand by his side and I chose to run away for love. Love that did nothing but torture me and nearly got me killed. I stumbled on a rock as the tears blurred my vision.

Kain reached out and grabbed me, stopping my fall and surrounding me in his warmth. He smelled so good; he always did. I turned my head to the side, comforted by the closeness of his lips. We couldn't be together, and my heart had never fully let him in, but at this moment in my life I needed someone on my side.

Kain's muscles twitched and his face fell. He didn't want to be this close to me, and that realization killed something inside my soul. I doubted our relationship would ever heal. This was all my fault.

"Let's go down there," Kain said, untangling our limbs and quickly leaving the path.

I followed, not sure if we were allowed to venture this close to the edge, but not willing to question him. After climbing over a few boulders, we found a flat spot overlooking one of the most beautiful places in the world.

"Wow," I breathed.

Kain sat and after a minute of wishing I had a camera, I joined him. The sun cast rays of light over the sharp rock outcroppings, but swallowed the crevices in pits of blackness. Ironic, I noticed, how the opposites complimented each other. I once thought that about Brendan. With me being a mermaid and he a selkie, we should have never been together. Still, he brought out the best in me, and I strived to be a better person. And because of that, I'd hurt everyone in my life.

"It was worth it," Kain said, breaking into my reflections after a lengthy stretch of silence.

Wondering if he referred to the risk he took coming to help me, my heart dropped when he continued.

"I'm glad Daniel made us stop. This is amazing."

I forced a smile and discreetly wiped my eyes. He didn't need to see me cry again. "Yeah, it's beautiful." Clearing my throat, I decided to broach the subject. "Are they going to accept me, Kain?"

He looked at me with sympathy and regret etched deep into his eyes. "I don't know."

"Can you tell me what happened? Did she force the shunning?" My mother, the clan leader at the time of my betrayal, had banned me for life. I don't think the full effect of that action had settled into my head before she was killed.

Kain rubbed his hands over his face then looked out over the massive canyon ridge. "She didn't want to do it."

I sucked in a breath. Those were the words I wanted to hear.

"Your father almost had her convinced," Kain continued. "He thought the drama would die down if she just ignored it for a few days."

"Did it?" I asked.

"No. Between my mother, your uncle, and some of the other clan leaders, she really didn't have a choice." He turned and faced me, eyes boring into my guilty conscience. "You didn't give her much of one."

Dropping my head, I swallowed hard. "What was your vote?"

"Eviana....don't." He shook his head.

"I need to know, Kain. Did you want me to be banned from our world?"

"Yes," he said, shocking me into reality. "If you were shunned, then I wouldn't have to see you again." He gazed off into the abyss. "I would've been forced to forget about you."

I couldn't breathe. Although I didn't deserve better, I hoped at least Kain would have fought for me. My mother had a duty for her people, and they always came first. I knew that the moment I made the decision to leave. But losing Kain's respect had been something I refused to contemplate. I'd been a fool. Another round of tears slipped down my cheeks.

"But I didn't vote for the shunning," Kain said, startling me out of my wallowing.

"What?"

"I couldn't do it. Everyone thought I was the biggest sucker of them all, but I couldn't vote for your banishment."

I didn't know what to say. For the millionth time in my life, I wondered why Kain put up with me. I certainly didn't deserve his friendship let alone his support. "Thank you," I whispered.

"Huh?"

"Thank you," I said again. Time stopped as we looked into each other's eyes and I relived every minute of my life with him. Our time coaching the young merfolk with their transitions, the trip to Florida, the night before I left. All memories darkened with the regret of my decision to leave with Brendan.

A piercing shriek echoed in my head as a screaming child ran off the path and directly toward us. In the distance his parent called out, warning him not to get too close to the edge. I watched in horror as the kid jumped from boulder to boulder, unaware of the danger.

Kain turned his head and I jumped to my feet just in time to watch the child leap onto the only rock sitting between him and the canyon. His parents were too far away to stop him.

Do not take another step! I forced the command outward from my body to his, hoping I had enough concentration to succeed. The boy wobbled, arms flailing, trying to decide what to do. When I saw his knee lift into the air, I knew he'd broken the control.

"Stop!" I yelled at him, not caring if the parents heard me or not. Kain started to run after the child, but it proved unnecessary. My compulsion succeeded this time, and I had full control over the boy's movements.

Without speaking, I directed my power to his feet, forcing him to jump off the boulder and walk toward Kain. In one swift move, Kain swept him up in his arms and turned to face me. I dropped my control, surprised I'd been able to focus the power.

Two terrified parents rushed around the rocks and screamed for their son. Kain nodded my way, then focused on reuniting the family. I didn't hear the conversation, but knew they were grateful for the help and ignorant to the reality of the situation.

A few minutes later, Kain walked back over to my side. "Good one," he said, and smiled at me. I grinned, not knowing if Kain understood how much his compliment meant to me. "Maybe we should go back to the parking lot and see if they're finished."

I nodded and followed him away from the canyon overlook. Leaving the sinister crevices behind, I concentrated on the radiance around me. At the end of darkness, there will be a light. At the end of this journey, I will be forced to face my actions. It won't be pleasant and it won't be easy, but at least I will have a friend by my side.

I could always count on Kain.

New Beginnings

As part of The Leila Marx Novels

Amber Garr

With one touch, she can see it all.

Leila is different. Her touch clairvoyant abilities set her apart from most, but she'll soon learn that she is not alone. When exploring the psychic community of her new city, she meets Terez. A true clairvoyant in every sense of the word, Terez quickly recognizes Leila's talents. In *Discovery*, Leila's first encounter with her mentor is nothing short of memorable.

Excited to be an entrepreneur, Mac overestimates his ability to hire an employee. Tired of interviewing humans, he uses his fae powers to keep himself entertained. That is, until Blake walks through the door. Reminding him of his past, Mac is thrilled to find one of his own. In *Human Resources*, Blake finds a new job while Mac finds a new friend.

For Janice - who loved to read and Candice - who loved to write. Thank you for the inspiration.

AN ANTHOLOGY

Discovery

The aroma of simmering bacon mixed with freshly cooked eggs filled the kitchen and tempted my stomach. Russ hustled back and forth between the table and stove as graceful as a dancer, not once breaking his stride. Much appreciated in my house, his cooking skills only added to the attractiveness.

I leaned against the counter to enjoy the view. Dressed only in a pair of jeans, Russ' bare back flexed with each little move. His muscular arms moved effortlessly and when he turned to smile at me, my heart fluttered.

"Good morning, beautiful," he said.

Despite the novelty of our relationship, I predicted he was here to stay. No one had ever made me feel like this before. I smiled and walked to his side, wrapping my arms around his waist and squeezing tight.

"Morning," I replied. Lifting my head to meet his lips, another rush of emotions flooded my body. On top of my own infatuation, an overwhelming sense of happiness embraced me. Despite trying to shield myself, Russ' feelings poured through every place our skin touched. We were both ridiculously content with each other. I smiled, but then noticed only one plate at the table. "You're not staying?"

Russ kissed the top of my head and pushed away to finish lifting the bacon out of the sizzling pan. "No, I have to go home and then into work for a bit."

Pouting, I pulled the chair out and sat down next to the single setting. He laughed and loaded up my plate.

"Don't look so sad. I'll be back tonight."

Rare for us to spend a night apart, I still couldn't control the tingling in my body every time we planned to see each other.

"What are you doing today?" Russ asked while rinsing the pans.

"I think I'll go check out that psychic I told you about." He'd cooked the bacon to a perfect crisp and I savored my first bite. With a full mouth, I added, "She's one of the last ones I haven't met."

Russ shook his head and chuckled. My little project amused him. Knowing the special gifts I had, he accepted the idea of others like me. But he thought my efforts to prove them wrong were unnecessary. Every time I moved to a new city, I made it a point of identifying the true psychics. So far, they've all been fake. In a city the size of Baltimore, I expected to find at least one. Maybe the lady today would be the real deal.

"Well, have fun." Russ dried his hands and leaned across the small kitchen table to grab my face. "As far as I'm concerned, you're the only psychic in my book."

"I'm not a full psychic," I pushed out between smooshed cheeks. My clairvoyant ability was limited to touch.

"Doesn't matter. You're mine."

The corner of his lips pulled up into a grin just before covering my mouth with his. I forgot about the delicious breakfast and my incessant need to find others like me, and lost myself in his touch. Minutes passed before we separated. I tried to pull him back, but he jumped out of the way, promising more later tonight.

Once he left, I prepared myself for the day. I grabbed the printed list of all the psychic ads in the city and suburban area. I'd knocked out the city list right away, and had now moved on to the suburban psychics.

The address put her close to a number of colleges and within a few miles of the city limits. A smart marketing tool. When I pulled up to the street, I couldn't help laugh at the flashing neon "Psychic Reading" sign. I pegged her as a fake for sure.

After parking halfway up the block, I almost fell back into my seat when I opened the car door. Something in the air felt dense and electrical. Chills developed along my arms and up my neck, making me suspicious of those around me.

Laughter drew my attention to the psychic's business. The dome-shaped home had a modest size front porch filled with ten college-aged girls. Sorority sisters I guessed, because of the matching sweatshirts and pink bows in their hair. The high pitched giggles intensified as I began to approach the house.

"You go first," one of the girls said. She nudged her friend who almost fell into the front door.

"No, you go," she laughed, slurring her words. Drunk on a Saturday morning. How I didn't miss college.

"It's your birthday," another girl chimed in.

The giggling and shoving continued as I walked closer to the front door. But I soon tuned it out, as the energy in the air began to suffocate me. This felt different than any of my other visits.

A door creaked open and the sorority girls fell silent. We all froze for a moment, until someone screamed and a giant gray cat ran out of the house and between their legs. Some of them jumped to the side, others squealed like it was a rat. A giant gray rat.

The cat made a beeline straight for me. Looking down at the creature sitting at my feet, it surprised me to find him staring back. "Hello," I said with a chuckle.

He answered with a noise that sounded like a purr and meow mixed together. I laughed again and bent forward to scoop him up into my arms. He weighed a ton, and just as I was about to ask who he belonged to, a small lady broke through the crowd of young girls.

Her graying long hair whipped around her shoulders in the wind, and a long green skirt and billowing purple blouse covered her tiny frame. We stared at each other for what seemed like minutes. The cat continued to purr as I stood still, unsure of what I felt. The tingling sensation subsided once the older lady smiled.

"Leila," she held out her arms. "Finally."

I looked behind me then back toward the lady and the girls. They seemed to sober up quick, and now watched our interaction with intent.

"Do I know you?" I asked the woman. She smiled and took a few steps closer to me, arms still spread. Maybe she wanted her cat. I held out the pet in my arms and pushed him in her direction. "He must belong to you?" I questioned.

"Yes," she replied. "And we've both been expecting you."

"Whoa," one of the girls said. "She's the real deal."

I leaned around the lady to look at the sorority sisters, thinking the exact same thing myself.

The woman turned around and acknowledged the girls. "I'm sorry ladies, but I'm closed today."

"Your sign says you're open," the loudest one replied.

"Well, I'm closed now."

"But we came all the way from Towson," she continued to push.

"If you come back next weekend, I'll give each of you a free reading." The woman's calm demeanor soothed each of us.

The girl nodded and herded her posse down the street, away from me, the giant cat, and the real psychic. Without saying a word, the woman lifted her cat from my hands and rubbed his head. The purrs intensified, making us smile and calming the environment.

"Why don't we go inside," she said.

"Wait, I don't even know your name."

She reached out and grabbed my hand before I could stop her. A bright light flashed behind my eyes and her energy surged through me. I saw the lady, smiling and laughing, as she sat on her porch with someone. Her animated face brought a familiar comfort that made me feel safe. Her hair flowed around her shoulders, blocking my view of the guest. She took a sip from the mug and tucked her hair behind her ear, revealing the other person. I saw myself sitting next to her, as though we were old friends, chatting the day away.

I jerked back my hand so fast I stumbled on the sidewalk. "How did you do that?" I gasped.

She smiled. "I showed you what is to come."

"I...I can't usually see the future."

"I passed the vision on to you. We are going to be great friends, Leila."

"I still don't know your name," I said. Even though I should have been fearful, my curiosity gained strength.

The woman continued walking to her house, beckoning me to follow. "I'm Terez," she finally said. I made it to the front door before she continued. "And you and I have a lot of catching up to do."

She stepped inside and flipped off her neon sign. The grey cat leaned over Terez's shoulder and called after me. Knowing this was what I'd come here to do, I decided to learn all that I could. Crossing the threshold, I sighed in relief. I'd finally found someone like me.

Human Resources

I set the three-page resume on my desk. "You do know what kind of store this is right, Mrs. Humphrey?" Looking at the meek little women sitting across from me, I shook my head. Her crocheted shawl, high collar blouse, and polyester trousers screamed nothing if not librarian.

And I wasn't hiring a librarian.

"It's a retail shop, Mr. Donahue." She glanced to the boxes of inventory stacked up along the edges of the store and arranged in neat aisles. "I've worked in retail stores all my life, and have experience in management."

In all fairness, she might not have interpreted the ad correctly. I wanted someone with experience, but probably not the kind she had.

I sighed. The store sign was in the back room and I didn't feel like walking all the way there. Estimating how quickly I could do this, I decided that Mrs. Humphrey could handle it. And if not, I would adjust her memory.

Taking in a sharp breath, I closed my eyes and envisioned the storage room. My body tingled for a split second before I snapped out of existence and materialized there. Picking up the signage, I popped back in front of Mrs. Humphrey holding the *Fantasy Villa* logo in my hands.

"Did you...did you just go somewhere?" she asked, clearly confused and a little concerned.

"No, Mrs. Humphrey. I only bent over to grab the sign. See?" I lifted it onto the counter. "This is the type of retail store I own."

It amused me to watch her expression as understanding sunk in. I think it was the phallic "V" that finally did it for her.

"Oh no, Mr. Donahue. I can't work here." As if noticing my attire for the first time, she turned up her nose. "I'm sorry...I...I have to leave."

She walked out of the store and I rubbed my temples. That was the fifth interview today. Didn't anyone need a job in Baltimore? Someone who wouldn't mind selling the kind of products I offered?

Another five candidates came and went. One was underage, two were so boring I flitted around the store a hundred times before they noticed anything weird going on. It didn't take more than a second to reset their memories. Another one seemed more attracted to me than the job. It happened sometimes with the fae. And the last guy proved to be a complete imbecile who got a little too excited about the employee discounts. A few times I popped up behind him, pretending to have my sword in hand, and then disappeared so quickly he only felt a slight breeze. I had to entertain myself somehow, and being around these ridiculous humans made me homesick for a land I left centuries ago.

My decision to leave home had not been an easy one. But after too many years of war, famine, and heartbreak, I needed a change. Living with the humans had been easy at first and I found my niche. I worked in brothels, speakeasies, and dance clubs. The years flew by as I utilized my talents to the best of my ability. Once I moved to Baltimore, I decided to open my own store, never realizing how difficult it would be to hire help.

Just as I was ready to give up for the day, and reconsider my options should I not find anyone, the door chimed. I stopped unpacking the boxes when I sensed a hint of familiarity that brought a smile to my face.

Someone had fae in their bloodline.

"Hello?" The new recruit called, unable to find me hidden amongst the inventory.

I materialized in front of him and found myself standing eye to eye with a young man, probably college age, although I was bad at guessing human years. He had spiked hair and wore tight black leather on every part of his body, mimicking my own outfit. I grinned when he stepped back a few feet.

"Did you just *appear* in front of me?" Despite the slight hint of fear in his voice, my entrance didn't seem to disturb him.

"Maybe," I teased. "Are you here to interview for the job?"

"Yes, sir."

"Do you know what kind of store this is?"

"I think so."

I cocked my head to the side, gauging his answer. In a blink, I popped over to the counter and then back in front of the young man, holding the store sign in my hand.

"Okay, you totally just did it again, didn't you?" he asked, this time more fascinated.

I smiled. "Maybe. This is the type of store I own."

"Whoa, that is the coolest artwork," he said, tracing his hand along each letter. "Who did this?"

"I did."

"Really? You have talent, man."

"Thank you. What's your name?"

"Blake," he said without taking his eyes off the sign.

"I'm Mac. When can you start?" He smelled like home to me. I guessed that a great-grandparent of his wasn't as human as the family thought. That happened sometimes with the fae. Humans find us irresistible, making self control difficult in times of need.

Blake smiled and slapped my shoulder. "Right away."

After hundreds of years moving from place to place, I finally planned to settle down and use my talents to the best of my ability in this world. Blake's supernatural connection comforted me, and I felt excited to supply a service to the humans as well.

"Okay, done. Why don't you start unpacking those boxes over…here," I said as I appeared next to a big pile of seasonal items.

He laughed. "All right. But can you teach me how to do that?"

"Probably not."

"Well that sucks," he said, opening the first box. "I would love to freak out my girlfriend with that trick."

"Perhaps there will be other things I can teach you then."

"Cool," Blake said with a nod, as we began the daunting task of unpacking my first adult entertainment store.

AN ANTHOLOGY

ABOUT THE AUTHOR

Amber Garr spends her days conducting scientific experiments and wondering if her next door neighbor is secretly a vampire. Born in Pennsylvania, she lives in Florida with her husband and their furry kids. Her childhood imaginary friend was a witch, Halloween is sacred, and she is certain she has a supernatural sense of smell. Amber is a Royal Palm Literary Award winner and author of *The Syrenka Series* and *The Leila Marx Novels*. When not obsessing over the unknown, she can be found dancing, reading, or enjoying a good movie.

Buy *The Syrenka Series* and *The Leila Marx Novels* on
Amazon, Barnes & Noble, and Smashwords.

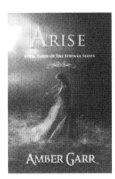

Learn more about Amber and her books at:
www.ambergarr.com
http://ambergarr.blogspot.com
Follow Amber on Twitter @AmberGarr1
Like Amber at: www.facebook.com – Author Page: Amber Garr

AN ANTHOLOGY

The Sound of Love

As part of The Kindrily Series

Karen Amanda Hooper

Once upon another lifetime, Mary was the most influential member of her kindrily. She and her soul mate, Nathaniel, are part of a family of kindred souls who live many lifetimes and retain centuries of memories through perpetual reincarnation. Like any couple in love, Mary and Nathaniel have their ups and downs. *The Sound of Love* is a glimpse into one of their past lives after tragedy strikes, leaving Nathaniel debilitated and Mary blaming herself.

For Aunt Pat, your strength and courage is inspiring. You are a true survivor.

AN ANTHOLOGY

The Sound of Love

The thwack was so loud it echoed for what felt like eternity. Nathaniel didn't make a sound. He reached for his head, fell to his knees, then toppled over before I could reach him.

"Oh, god!" I yelled, trying to keep my balance. "I forgot to shout *jibe*. I'm so sorry!"

The sailboat groaned as it rocked from side to side, and the boom creaked as it continued swinging through the air. I hauled in the jib sheet, let out the mainsheet, and steadied us.

"Are you alright?" I asked, rushing to Nathaniel's side. I rolled him onto his back. His eyes were closed, and his body was limp, but he managed a groan. "I'm so sorry, my love. I'm a genuine dolt. Please forgive me."

Nathaniel had sustained too many injuries to count throughout our lifetimes. This wasn't his first, and I was certain it wouldn't be his last, but it was entirely my fault.

Then I saw the blood. Blood trickling out of his ears was a first.

I wanted to call out for help, but given the fact we were alone, and so far out to sea that I couldn't see land, shouting for help was useless.

I ripped off my sweater, tore it in half, and pressed both pieces against the side of his head.

This too shall pass. I mentally repeated it over and over, hoping Nathaniel's injury wasn't as bad as my crumbling heart made it out to be. He didn't fight me when I pressed the material more firmly. He barely flinched.

"Does it hurt?" I asked him. Of course it hurt. What a daft question. His eyes rolled back in his head, so I nudged him. "Nathaniel. Nathaniel!"

He fluttered back to consciousness.

"How bad is the pain?"

His blank stare confirmed my fear.

I cursed under my breath then spoke to him, over emphasizing each of my words. "You can't hear me. Can you?"

He barely shook his head, but that was enough. The blow to the back of his skull had caused serious damage. Hopefully his inability to hear me was only temporary. The blood was what worried me. What if his brain was hemorrhaging or something more horrible?

"I should have insisted you listen to me. I told you the Titanic sinking last week was a clear indicator that sea voyage wasn't favorable. Why didn't I follow my bloody instincts?" I felt his pulse. A tad bit weaker than usual, but still steady. Nathaniel was shivering, so I pulled him tight against my chest and said a silent prayer. Then I realized prayers weren't going to help us get back to land any quicker.

Our normal recourse for escaping dire situations was out of the question; there was no way Nathaniel could use his power right now. Even if he had enough energy to teleport to a hospital, the traversing would drain what was left of him and he'd probably lose consciousness altogether. I had to get him back to land and seen by a doctor. I glanced around, assessing the boat and hoping I remembered enough to sail us home by myself.

"Brilliant anniversary celebration," I shouted to him as I ripped the blanket out from under the picnic he had set up for us. Plates, biscuits, and chocolate petit fours rolled around the deck in every direction. "The moon has been wreaking havoc on the planet all month. The planets were perfectly aligned for us to attract tragedy, and here we are. Maybe next year you'll listen to me, yes?"

If he could listen to me. He'd need his ears to be functioning in order to listen. "Dear universe," I begged aloud, "please don't let him be deaf."

I wrapped the blanket around him and placed a life vest under his head, then used my scarf to tie the pieces of my sweater in place over his ears. I smoothed his long bangs away from his face. "Please stop bleeding. I'd prefer this life be a lengthy one. I'm not ready for you or me to die yet. Understand?"

He didn't respond, or open his eyes, but I had to keep talking. Whether he could hear me or not, it made me feel less alone. With Nathaniel by my side, I could do anything. Even if he was passed out on the deck of the sailboat, he was still with me. I could navigate us out of this mess, and back to port. I could and I would.

"Right then," I said, grabbing the ship's wheel and staring up at the windless sky. If I focused hard enough, I could see stars shining even through the daylight. I zeroed in on the one that would guide us home. The ship was becalmed and eerily quiet. "Tallyho, shall we?"

I glanced back at Nathaniel, unmoving, bleeding, and silent. "Yes," I nodded with determination. "Glad you agree."

~

Dr. Wright closed his black bag and stood to leave. "Yes, I'm certain the hearing loss is permanent, but the amnesia was short-term and seems to have dissipated."

I glanced at Nathaniel, awake and alert in bed, then I leaned closer to the doctor, tilting my head so Nathaniel couldn't hear me, or see my lips. "Perhaps he's faking? He's always been keen on practical jokes."

Dr. Wright smirked. "We both know Nathaniel wouldn't fake such a thing."

"Sadly, you are right. But, what do we do? I mean what happens next?" I smoothed down my dress, unsure of what to do with my hands, feeling helpless because I couldn't fix the situation.

"It's like any other disability. People learn to live with it."

That was his best medical advice? Learn to live with it? A frustrated sigh whooshed out of me like a gale force wind. I couldn't make Nathaniel better. No one could make him hear again. I kissed Nathaniel's forehead and pointed toward the door then made a walking motion with my fingers. He started to pull back his covers.

"No!" I shouted, as if he'd hear me if I could just be loud enough. I pressed on his chest. "I'll see the doctor out." Ridiculously, I spoke loud and slow again. "You stay in bed and rest."

He nodded then looked past me, waving goodbye to Dr. Wright.

At the front door, I thanked the doctor and asked if there was anything I could do to increase Nathaniel's chances of regaining his hearing. "I don't believe so, but keep paper and pen handy so you can communicate. Mrs. Caldwell of Kensington teaches sign language and comes highly recommended."

"Yes, Mrs. Caldwell. Lovely. I'll ring her in the morning." It wouldn't be the first time Nathaniel and I had to learn a new language, but signing would be a first.

"Good evening, Mary." Dr. Wright tipped his hat and strolled down the pathway.

I went inside, rummaged through drawers until I found a notepad and pen, and returned to our bedroom. The bed was empty.

"Nathaniel!" I called out. I rolled my eyes at my own repetitive stupidity. "He can't hear you," I mumbled to myself. "He's deaf."

My heart weakened again at the thought. He'd never hear music again. Never hear birds chirping. Never hear the cries of our baby—if we ever had children. The bathroom door opened and he smiled at me.

"How can you smile at a time like this?"

His brow furrowed. "What?"

Frustrated, I wrote on the notepad. *You're deaf but smiling.*

I held it up for him to read. His eyes scanned the page and he shrugged. "When I first came to, I didn't know who you were." He was speaking differently than normal. His words were more drawn out and he spoke slower. "I didn't know who I was. I was terrified. I'm grateful my memories returned so quickly. Isn't that a proper cause for happiness?"

I turned away, guiltily pacing the room. His amnesia had been terrifying. Nathaniel and I had acquired and retained multiple lifetimes of memories, centuries of precious moments and details that compiled our lengthy volumes of history together. If his memory had been permanently damaged it would have undone me.

In my peripheral vision, I saw Nathaniel vanish.

"Bloody hell!" I stomped my foot, angry that he'd traverse so soon after his injury. Teleporting required a lot of energy, and he'd barely been out of bed five minutes. I kept pacing, twirling my ring around my finger, willing him to come home immediately.

I grabbed the pad, sat in our bedside chair and wrote, *It's all my fault.*

I continued writing the same sentence over and over. I had written *It's all my fault* twelve times when Nathaniel reappeared in front of me.

"Where on earth did you go?"

He bowed his head and from behind his back, he pulled a singled beautiful peacock feather. "A reminder that everything happens for a reason."

"Don't use my own words and beliefs against me right now."

He squinted, clearly not sure what I had said.

I pushed the feather aside and held up my page, filled with the ugly truth. It was all my fault.

He read it and chuckled. "That it is."

"You're laughing?" I wrote furiously. *I feel wretched!*

"I forgive you."

"No!" It shouldn't have been that easy. Not in this situation. I scribbled as fast as I could. *It's permanent. You're never going to hear again because of me!*

He lowered his chin and raised one brow. "Nothing is permanent for us. I will hear again. You know that."

How could he be so nonchalant about such a debilitating injury? If I hadn't forgotten to shout out to him when I jibed then the boom would have never struck him. My carelessness deprived him of one of his basic and most used senses. I wrote with a heavy heart, *Not in this lifetime.*

He shrugged. "Lives are short. This one will be over before you know it."

What will I tell the rest of our kindrily? They will be devastated.

"They will no doubt find it humorous, and tease you about it for many lives to come. You might want to thicken your skin."

I shook my head, fighting back guilty tears. The lovely peacock feather on the floor became a blur of blue and green. Yes, I believed everything—no matter how bad it seemed—happened for a reason. But I also believed in following my intuition, listening to the stars when they whispered warnings and guided me along specific paths. They had warned me not to get on that boat and I didn't listen. We shouldn't have been sailing. Yet even then, I could have simply remembered to shout when I released the sail. I began to write again, but Nathaniel placed his hand on my pen and motioned for me to give him the pad, so I did.

He tossed it on the bed and took my hands, pulling me close to him, then lifted my chin. "Breathe."

Why was he trying to calm me? He should have been angry. He should have been upset with me. He pointed to his eyes. Our eyes were the windows to our souls. I gazed into his beautiful green abyss and saw the deep love and calmness he felt. Not a speck of anger, not a fleck of irritation.

I spoke slowly. "I'll never forgive myself."

"That's nonsense. I forgave you the moment it happened."

"But you shouldn't. You—"

He silenced me by placing his fingers on my lips. His fingertips trailed down my chin and along my neck. "Tell me."

"Tell you what?" I knew what he wanted me to say, but it didn't feel like the appropriate time.

"All is and will be exactly as it should be. A brilliant woman shared that bit of wisdom with me on several occasions, and it's worth repeating."

My words, recited back at me when I needed them most. Perhaps, as awful as it seemed, Nathaniel losing his hearing truly was in the cards. If so, nothing I could have done would have stopped it. If it hadn't happened on a sailboat, fate would have forced it to happen in some other manner. Nothing to be done except accept it, and, as the good doctor said, *learn to live with it.*

Nathaniel continued to stare at me. We could have filled a dozen notepads and still not been able to communicate what the volumes of forgiveness and adoration in his eyes were revealing.

He leaned in and kissed me. No matter how many different lives we lived, no matter how many bodies we inhabited, or how long we'd been together, his kisses never lost their magical effect.

He lightly stroked my neck. "Tell me."

My throat tightened. He wouldn't hear me speak his favorite words again. At least not until our next life. And even then, how could we be sure I hadn't created some ripple effect when each life he'd be born with no hearing?

"Tell me," he repeated in a whisper.

"I love you." His fingertips rested against my throat, making me aware of the vibration of my vocal chords. "Then, now, and eternally."

His smile stretched so big it almost filled the room. "See, I don't need to hear the words. I can feel the love between us."

My Nathaniel. Always forgiving. Forever the optimist. "Happy Anniversary, Mary," he said. "This will be one for the memory books."

"I'd prefer to erase all recollection of this day—for good."

"Not a chance." With one finger, he traced our signature figure eight around my eyes. "No erasing permitted, even the not-so-glorious moments."

I picked up the notepad and chuckled at myself as I wrote, *Next life, we stay far away from boats. Perhaps we could live in the desert.*

Nathan wrapped his arms around my waist and pulled me tight against him. "Sounds perfect."

AN ANTHOLOGY

ABOUT THE AUTHOR

Karen Hooper was born and bred in Baltimore, frolicked and froze in Colorado for a couple of years and is currently sunning and splashing around Florida with her two beloved dogs. She's addicted to coffee, chocolate, and complicated happily-ever-afters.

Buy *Grasping at Eternity* on Amazon and Barnes and Noble.

Learn more about Karen and her books at:
http://www.karenamandahooper.com
Follow Karen on Twitter @Karen_Hooper
Like Karen at http://www.facebook.com/AuthorKaren

AN ANTHOLOGY

FURTHERMORE

Rapture

As Part of the Saga of the Setti Series

Stephanie Judice

Muirne's Melody

1352 A.D.—Muirne is a slave in the land of Icelandic barbarians. Captured from her Celtic clan, she now serves in the home of Torvald—watchful and silent. On this night's gathering, her angelic voice and beauty entrances everyone, especially her master. Torvald's desire sets her on a path toward her true destiny, one that will bind her to a green-eyed stranger and a perilous future. As a dark evil approaches, Muirne is given the power of a Sounder, the first one to ever walk the earth.

Jeremy's Heart

PRESENT DAY—Jeremy is the cocky, confident Sounder of Homer's clan. Nothing can touch Jeremy, or so they think. Behind the suave, swaggering exterior, there are fractures threatening to pull him apart. The lack of love as a child, the loss of a dear friend, and the unknown future loom before him as the Setti prepare for the next battle with the Reapers. The last thing he expected at this point in his life was . . . love.

Fall from Grace

NEAR FUTURE—Sveigja was once a Setti, having lost the right to call himself a soldier of light. He walks in the dark, accepting its cold embrace. For over a millennium, he has been content with his loss, with his lot, but meeting the Guardian Clara has changed things. She reminds him of himself before the change, before the darkness. Recognizing this aching feeling inside, he does not want to go on alone. He longs for a future where he no longer bends his knee to the King of Beasts, Bolverk. He wants the crown for himself. Now he must find a way to win Clara's obedience by persuasion or by force.

In memory of my grandmother, Anna Bess Smith
and
For Joyce Lamothe, a second mother to me in childhood
who first taught me to love books.

Muirne's Melody

Muirne's milk-pale skin and flaxen hair glowed golden in the hearth's light. She stood, poised at the head of the hall, hands clasped at the small of her back. All eyes fixed on her, especially Torvald's. No one could turn away from such beauty—in body and song. Her voice lifted, lilted, then chorused in a lament of loss and longing.

"The hills will howl, and echo my love—
of a place where winds won't die—
The fire will burn, warming my heart—
in a place where I never cry."

Torvald watched her from the head of the feast table like a lion would his prey. He leaned casually to one side, the bulk of him almost too big for the chair. His well-muscled body itched for a little action, and his eyes rested where he might find it.

He was proud of his captive from across the sea. She was a lovely girl with a lovely voice, slowly blossoming into a woman. He had noticed. He would take her as his own soon enough, as a wife.

Marriage with slaves was not common, but he would be forgiven. One only need look at her to understand his willingness to forego custom. Still, he did not want to spoil her too early.

He remembered his father's words from long ago on the subject of women: 'Pluck her too quick, and the flower will wilt.' He did not want his flower to wilt. Not yet. When she sang, she was radiant. His neighbor clansmen envied his possession, and he liked that.

The firelight framed her womanly figure like a halo, twisting his thoughts. Her clear blue eyes never rested on him for long—too skittish. He liked that, too. A little fear would keep her submissive, pliant.

Her voice lifted again in a mournful tone, carrying across the great hall of the longhouse.

"The sea will wave—

and the birds will fly—

to a faraway home of their own."

He pondered what Celtic man had let such a jewel wander from home, chaperoned only by an old hag. Great fortune for him. The bright jewel amused him and his guests quite nicely. His eyes skimmed down her frame. He longed for more private amusement. His father's words seemed unimportant now. She was ripe enough for the picking. He'd waited far longer than any other man would have.

When the song ended, Torvald led the room in raucous shouts and cheers. His barrel-chested neighbor, Ragna, slapped Torvald companionably on the shoulder.

"That's a fine one you caught there, Torvald."

"I know," he agreed, gazing intently upon his prize.

"But I tell you, my friend," said Ragna, "As I said before, there is talk. Invaders from the North, perhaps."

Ragna was landowner of the farmstead just south of Torvald.

"What talk?" he asked.

"I've heard it, too, from the blacksmith in the village," said Grímarr, a gaunt, beady-eyed merchant.

"What does he say? What are you going on about?"

"Shadows. Men disguised, lurking about and spying on the village," replied Grímarr.

"Nonsense," said Torvald. "If invaders wanted our land, they wouldn't creep about. They'd be upon us like a storm."

"My slave heard that peasant woman in town speak of nightmares and dragons, the world ending in fire."

"Who? The redhead?"

Grímarr grunted agreement.

"That witch," groaned Torvald. "She needs to get a man and be quick about it so she has something better to do than stir up trouble."

They all threw their heads back in laughter. Ragna's daughter offered the men more barley ale, brushing up against Torvald suggestively. He glanced once more at Muirne then turned to the voluptuous, young woman at his side, grabbing her around the hips and giving a squeeze.

❦ ❦ ❦

Muirne stood quietly in the corner. She had noticed her master's burning gaze from across the room. Ragna's fat daughter refilled his cup, flirting shamelessly until his attention finally turned to the young brunette. Torvald would be a catch for any woman as the owner of the largest farmstead in the province of Thorndanes. Muirne shivered, knowing her master's eyes roved too long on her.

She longed to be dismissed or to sing again. When she sang, she saw none of them. In her mind's eye, she envisioned her homeland—the rumbling laughter of her Da, the sweet smile of her sister Moira, the gentle hand of her mama.

Her wistful thoughts of home always conjured a melancholy melody. The onlookers would only think of their own loved ones gone to sea or voyages still to come far away from these familiar shores. They would never think Muirne's voice echoed a sorrow she could not endure for much longer.

"Muirne, you look pale. You need something to eat," said the cook, Inga, having set another plate of bread and cheese on the feast table. "Come with me."

"But, Master Torvald may wish for another song."

"He'll be heavy into his ale soon enough. I'll take the blame. Come now."

"Thank you, Inga."

Inga had been born a slave in the family under Torvald's grandfather. She had been the cook for the household long before Muirne had come into it. Though small and angular, she had strong arms and always moved swiftly and with purpose.

"You have such a fine voice, dear heart, but you wear yourself out singing for those brutes," said Inga, ushering her into the kitchen and onto a stool.

Muirne loved the kitchen. It smelled of meat and spice and was always warm. Inga poured a cup of mead, scraped a mound of *skyr* onto a wooden plate with a slice of brown bread and pushed it in front of Muirne.

"Eat."

Muirne scooped a mouthful of the creamy, white cheese onto a corner of the bread, taking a small bite. She was always eager to please Inga, her only parental figure in this new, cold world. Muirne hoped her mother, father, and sister were still living peacefully on their own farm back home across the waters.

She would never forget the fateful day last year when she left home with her widowed aunt to go to market in a nearby coastal village. The day of their arrival marked the last day the little village would exist. When foreign ships washed ashore, Norse raiders stormed the village, stealing everything of value and burning the rest. Torvald took many slaves, including Muirne. Her aunt had died trying to defend her. Muirne went quietly, as usual. Always the obedient girl, even into slavery.

"Where are you, girl? Come back to me," snapped Inga.

"I am sorry. My mind is wandering so much today."

"Well, you can eat while your mind wanders. Eat up."

Muirne did as she was told, knowing Inga only wanted her well-fed. Inga flitted around the kitchen, fetching a bowl of broth from the pot over the fire. She placed it gently in front of Muirne.

"What's wrong, my dear? I can tell when something is worrying you."

"I've been thinking of home again."

Inga's high brow bunched up. Her gnarled fingers went to work, slapping a mound of dough on the wooden table and kneading it with her knuckles. The rhythmic sound of her pounding and kneading soothed Muirne—a pleasant, domestic sound.

"No need thinking of that," she said curtly, "best to move on. If you hold onto dreams, they'll break your heart. You and I, people like us, we've no business with dreams."

She took a knife and cut the flattened dough into a dozen pieces, rolling them into small loaves. She seemed to speak from a distant hurt. Muirne wondered what loss she had suffered to make her so bitter.

"I'm tired, Inga. I think I'll go to bed."

Inga paused in her baking, stepping over to a wooden chest in the corner.

"Best take this then," she said, handing her a coarse, woolen blanket along with the crust of bread she had not yet finished. "You'll need an extra one tonight. A storm's brewin'."

Muirne took the blanket and crept through the great hall of the longhouse, cringing as she walked past the boisterous men and cackling women, wishing she had thought to use the back door leading from the kitchen. She tried not to draw anyone's eye. She nearly made it to the door when a booming voice called behind her.

"Muirne!" shouted Torvald. "Wait."

She paused and turned, chin down and head bowed. She glanced sideways to see the men at the table grinning as Torvald made his way to her.

"You are leaving too early, Muirne," he said, his deep voice brushing against her with scorn.

"I am tired, master."

He fingered the woolen blanket she held in her delicate arms. She only came up to his chest. She knew he was considered a specimen of worth—brawny and strong with the fair looks of his kind. But everything about him frightened her. When she looked at him, she saw him wielding the sword against her people. She saw blood and death and loss. Even now, he still wore a thin, war-braid alongside one temple from the last raid across the waters. In her mind, he would always have blood-stained hands.

"Will this keep you warm?" he asked in a low, gruff voice. He tipped her chin up, forcing her to look into his gray eyes. "*I would like to keep you warm, Muirne.*"

Her heart hammered. She wanted to run, scream, anything. Silence was her only reply. He smiled, taking this as some sort of acceptance. Or perhaps, he didn't care whether she accepted or not. She was his property after all.

He unfolded the blanket and draped it around Muirne's shoulders, leaning very close to her. She wanted to step back away from him, but she knew better. He pulled one of her hands from her side, placing the folds of the fabric between her fingers. His keen watchfulness made her pulse speed up erratically. Her heart felt like a bird trapped in a too-small cage. She looked down again, unable to keep his steely gaze.

"This rough blanket does not suit you, Muirne. You should be wrapped in fine fabrics and bedding."

Until this moment, he had always kept his distance, kept his lust only in his eyes, never allowing it to slip over. Why he had decided to cross the invisible line tonight, she did not know.

"Do not go to sleep when you get to your quarters," he commanded, smoothing a lock of her golden hair between his fingers. "Not yet."

His promise, or threat, lingered heavily between them.

"Did you hear me, Muirne?"

His fingers wrapped around the back of her neck, tilting her chin up forcefully with his thumb. She hitched her breath in sharply, trembling at the wicked gleam in his gray eyes. She nodded, unable to make a sound.

"Good," he said, so close as he stroked his thumb along her windpipe.

A shout of laughter called Torvald's attention. He finally let her go and stepped abruptly away, rejoining his company. Muirne caught the slit-eyed glare of Ragna's fat daughter just before she shut the door to the great hall. She desperately wished Torvald liked his women thick and dark-haired.

The wind bit at her ankles as she shuffled quickly to the small outbuilding where she slept. The boy who cared for the dogs, sheep, and cattle was not on his straw mattress on the floor. He should be sound asleep by now. Bretta was still in the great hall, helping serve the men. All three of them had been taken the same day from that coastal village. The boy had not spoken one word during all this time in captivity.

Muirne sat on the small raised bed she shared with Bretta. She could not move, knowing Torvald would be coming soon, knowing what he would be coming for. She trembled, wringing her hands in her lap. She thought of her parents—their loving embrace, the soft touches, the gentle smiles. She could not imagine Torvald treating her so gently, so kindly.

A tear slid down her face, dropping onto her hand. Her father's face came to mind. She remembered sitting on his lap in front of the fire at home. His words haunted her now.

"One day, my love, when it comes time for handfasting, I will be the one to tie the first ribbon. But *I* will choose the man. You will have only the best kind of man, one worthy of my little Sunflower."

A sob caught in her throat. If her poor father knew what would become of his Sunflower. To be reduced to a slave, a toy for Norsemen to leer at. To become the worst kind of woman, kept for the pleasure of a foreign beast. One word escaped her lips—loud and clear in the small, silent room.

"No."

She wiped the tears away with the back of her hand, seeing her heavy, hooded cloak on the hook by the door. She noticed the pair of sheep-skin boots fashioned by the boy for her. He refused to speak, but would communicate with gifts of this kind. Instantly, she was up and moving. With boots and cloak fastened, she crept outside, pulling the hood up to hide her mane of golden hair.

No one lingered behind the main longhouse. The wind was biting cold. The night chased everyone indoors to find warmth. A rumble of laughter rolled from the great hall. The ale kept them busy. Good. She still had time. Without a plan except to flee as far and as fast as she could, she slipped past the dog-pen, tossing a piece of crusty bread from Inga's dinner to keep them quiet. She headed north.

Muirne climbed the steep hill on the lee side of the farmstead. Icy wind whipped and pulled at her cloak as if pushing her off her current course. Head down, she pressed on, her breath frosting the air. The hills dipped and rolled. She trudged on as best she could.

She had heard of a kind landowner to the northeast with a large sheep farm. It was rumored around the village that he owned no slaves. He was a mystery, this lone man in the hills. Perhaps he would give her shelter for one night before she moved on.

There was no moon. Dark clouds snuffed out what little light the starry sky usually provided. Muirne shivered, trying to keep up her pace. A stinging, misty rain whirled around her skirts.

"Goddess Danu, please protect me from these elements," she whispered into the wind. "Do not let me perish this way."

The mist suddenly turned to snow, still stinging her cheeks and exposed fingers. She wondered if this was the cruel answer to a desperate prayer. She thought she heard the barking of dogs over the hills. Pressing forward over the next down, she saw a faint silhouette of a circle of standing stones in the distance. Something flashed darkly in her peripheral vision. She jerked sideways to see what it was. Nothing. Nothing but wind and snow.

"You cannot lose your mind, Muirne. Not now."

A gust screamed over the down, tugging the hood off her head. Tendrils of hair pulled loose, tangling around her face. The stinging gale seemed to be pushing her away from this place, but she kept moving. She could not go back.

Mounting the hill where the circle of monoliths stood like sentinels in the night, she definitely heard the distant barking of dogs. Torvald.

She fell to her knees, reciting every prayer she knew.

"Gods of the Sidhe, of heaven and earth, God of the Hebrew and the Christian—wherever you are, hear me now. Save me, and I will be your servant and do all that you ask of me."

The wind suddenly stopped howling. An eerie silence fell. Snow drifted softly. Muirne looked up in wonder, then a sudden, brilliant flash of light appeared. The light came not from above but from within her own bosom. Rays of purple, pink, gold, and indigo beamed outward. A burning sensation pierced Muirne's heart. Ribbons of color cocooned her in a warmth she had never felt before, filling her to the core.

She cried out in shock, wailing into the wind. Her voice reverberated over the hills and into the night. Vibrations of sound shook her whole body until she crumbled to the earth, wracked with a strange sensation tingling through her frame. The light vanished in a snap. She quivered with an energy unknown to her. Silence.

What happened? She did not know. But she was no longer cold, no longer afraid. What a strange answer to a pleading prayer. What could this mean?

Minutes elapsed as she breathed slow and deep in this new solitude—one where she did not feel alone. She could not move, basking in this strange sensation.

Outside the standing stones, a figure of a man approached in the falling snow, holding something small and furry in his arms. He placed the tiny creature on the ground as he knelt beside Muirne. She could not make out his features at first, until he drew closer. Gentle green eyes gazed down. He had a pleasing face though it was fixed in a grave expression. Somehow, she was not afraid of him.

"I came out in this cold to find my lost lamb and ended up finding two," said the young man. "Come, little lamb, we must get you inside."

She tried to protest, but he lifted her with ease into his arms. The tingling sensation had subsided, yet his warmth comforted her.

"Are you injured? I heard someone scream."

Muirne shook her head. She could not tell this stranger what had happened to her. She did not know herself.

"What about your lamb?" she asked, thinking of the poor creature.

"I will come back for her."

He carried her down the hill away from the standing stones when the sound of baying hounds drew close. The man looked at her, frowning.

"Are the hounds for you?" he asked.

"Yes."

Muirne would never lie.

"You should leave me here," she added. "It will be bad if he finds me with you."

The stranger continued to walk on, even with the hounds drawing closer and closer.

"I will not abandon you," he promised with a determined expression on his face. "You are a slave?"

She nodded. She knew the Norse tongue now, but spoke the language in a soft, lilting manner, betraying her as a foreigner. The dogs were directly upon them.

"Stop!" bellowed a familiar voice.

Muirne whimpered. The stranger cradled her closer. He turned, holding her tightly in his arms, like a treasure he would not give up.

"I know you," grumbled Torvald, holding the reins to his pack of dogs.

Ragna, the skinny one, and several other men from the feast stood on either side of him. Torvald's eyes blazed wild and fierce. Muirne could not look at him.

"Put her down and go back to your sheep, Leif. She is my property, and I don't like your hands on her," he spat, words laced with malice.

Muirne looked up at Leif, his jaw clenching, his eyes unreadable. He set her down gently. She almost felt relief, not wanting danger to come to this man. He seemed too kind to die for her, for a slave. He then pushed her behind him, blocking her from the men.

"It seems you've lost your property. I found her. She's mine now."

Muirne did not like this talk, as if she were a bauble to pass between men. But there was something in the tone of her strange savior that sounded very different from Torvald's. He did not look at her in the same way either. She leaned closer to his back, instinctually knowing she was safe with him. She pressed her cheek to his sheepskin coat.

Torvald laughed. His brutish band of men did the same.

"I have no problem fighting for my slave. Come on then, boy. Let's see what you can do."

Muirne looked out into the night, wishing she were somewhere else, wishing this was not her lot. Dark shadows flitted across her vision, and then vanished. She looked again. Something moved in the night. She felt a presence she could not see. A malevolent energy lingered in this place.

Leif stepped forward. Torvald handed the reins to Ragna. He circled Leif, crunching new-fallen snow. Though still cast in shadow, Muirne could see the kind stranger better now. Well-built, brown hair to his shoulder, as tall as Torvald, but not as thick.

Torvald pulled his short-sword from under his calf-skin coat. Muirne's heart plummeted. The fact that he'd brought such a weapon to recapture his wayward slave chilled her bone-deep. His gray eyes found her, revealing all the fury she had incited in one swift glance. She trembled, having lost the tranquility she had found moments before.

Torvald dove and swung his sword, arcing toward the farmer's neck. Leif swiveled behind him, kicking him to the ground. Torvald rolled but Leif was on top, pounding his face. The farmer's rage, sudden and fierce, seemed to stem from more than this moment.

"Get him, Torvald," shouted Ragna, inching forward.

The dogs barked in a frenzy. Muirne cowered backward. She sensed a dark presence among them as did the hounds. The clouds parted, letting the light of the moon filter through. Then she saw them.

A dozen tall, black figures melted out of the shadows behind Ragna and the other men. Their skin glistened, reminding Muirne of the scales of fish. She remembered her mother's tales of the selkies—

mystical seal-like creatures who sometimes walked the earth among humans. Could these creatures be related to the shapeshifters of old? She froze in fear.

The dogs yelped and growled, turning away from the men.

"Gods above," whispered Muirne, staring at the black, scaly-skinned figures with glowing yellow eyes peering menacingly from the dark.

Two of them raced forward and grasped Ragna's shoulders. The oafish man's face contorted, eyes widened in fear. The other dark creatures crept forward, all of them putting hands on the other men. Each man stiffened with their touch, freezing where they stood with expressions of agony, unable to speak.

"No!" Muirne yelled, pulling Leif's attention away from Torvald gripped in a death struggle beneath him.

The farmer followed Muirne's gaze. The dogs whimpered and growled at the empty air. Torvald used the distraction to club Leif across the jaw and scramble to his feet. Muirne stared at the horror before her eyes. The dogs yelped and fled into the night, abandoning their masters.

"What is wrong with them?" asked Leif, bewildered as to why Ragna and the others stood like statues with woeful looks on their faces.

"You do not see them?" asked Muirne, her voice shaking.

Confused, Torvald stared at his men in petrified shock. The shadow creatures did not move. They seemed to be waiting for something. A crackling sound splintered the night. Muirne looked up the hill to the circle of standing stones. Lightning threaded between two of the taller pillars, snapping visibly in a web of splintered light.

"By Odin," muttered Leif, "what devilry is this?"

Muirne gasped, pointing up the hill. An ominous wave of evil thickened the air just as a demonic beast stepped from nothingness between the pillars. The body resembled the shape of a man, though twice the size in height and girth. Its dark, greenish-black skin rippled with some unseen energy rolling beneath it. A strange cloak draped its massive shoulders. Two serpentine, yellow eyes glowed from a malformed face. A knotty, hairless head turned toward the group below. The beast whipped out pointed wings. One hand flexed seven long fingers; the other arm was a sharpened blade of black bone. The creature began descending the hill coming directly toward them in long, steady strides.

"It cannot be," whispered Leif.

"You witch!" Torvald hissed. "What have you brought upon us?"

Muirne shook her head, unable to believe her eyes. Some force stirred deep inside Muirne, compelling her to scream at the top of her lungs. She did so. The same burning sensation she felt moments after her prayer swelled in her breast. A crackling noise near the throng of statue-like men drew Leif's attention. Her voice had broken their cloaking shields, revealing them to the naked eye.

Leif gasped, stepping toward Muirne in a protective stance, finally seeing the shadow creatures with their hands clamped on the shoulders of the other men. Torvald fled into the night at once. Muirne grabbed Leif's hand, pulling him backward. The shadow men hissed at Muirne, knowing she held some power against them.

Their beastly master came closer, ignoring the terrified humans watching the scene, and plunged his bone-blade into the chest of Ragna. The dying man screamed in pain, finally finding his voice. The large man that once terrified Muirne with his fierceness transformed into stone as the life was sucked out of him by the demon's blade.

A banshee cry shrieked from above. More of the beasts stepped from the web of electricity alongside a different, shriveled creature with ashy wings and no facial features at all but a gaping mouth.

"Come!" yelled Muirne. "We must go!"

Leif held her hand tightly and ran. Screams and cries filled the night behind them as he pulled her faster and faster away from this place. Muirne's legs became tangled in her skirts. She fell in the snow. Leif lifted her into his arms, carrying her swiftly away. The cries grew distant, faint, and then they heard nothing but the whoosh of the soft wind.

"You can put me down. You must be tired," said Muirne, still clasping him about the neck.

"We're almost there," he said, slowing to a swift march.

They walked a short distance into a woodland where a longhouse appeared suddenly before them. Muirne could not help but think this home seemed hidden away from the world. Smoke furled from the sod chimney at the top. Leif quickly opened the door and closed it, setting her down. A black sheepdog lifted its head from a woolen pallet near the hearth.

"Go to the fire. Take off your cloak. You need to get warm," he said curtly, disappearing into a chamber set apart from the main room.

This house was half the size of Torvald's hall, but what need had a sheep farmer for a large house. He did not entertain. Muirne wondered if he ever saw anyone at all, so isolated in these woods. She did as she was told, moving close to the fire. The big dog licked her hand. She patted his head, and he curled up again on his bed.

The room was warm and smelled of tallow. Braided candle wicks hung near the far wall. A table along the back of the room was lined with jars, one of which had sticks of cinnamon sticking out of the top. Muirne had never known a man to do such things for himself. But there was no other person in sight, other than the friendly dog, well-cared for and sleeping soundly on a bed of wool.

Still in shock, she wrapped her arms around herself and moved to the fire. Leif appeared again, handing her a soft, dry blanket. He hung her wet cloak on a hook in the wooden mantle above the fire, as well as his own.

"Come. Sit," he commanded, though his tone was gentler than Torvald's.

She sat in a chair near the fire as he pulled up another next to her. In the warm glow of the room, Muirne realized he had a more than pleasing face. She became wary, alone with a man so handsome and so young. Yet his demeanor was not frightening or threatening. Quite the contrary. He leaned forward, his elbows on his knees, his head in his hands.

Muirne found her voice.

"You did not imagine what we saw," she said. "Those demons. They are real, and I am not a witch who conjured them."

Leif lifted his head, his green eyes searching her own. His expression softened. Her heart sped up again, but the feeling was far different from her earlier experience. This was not fear.

"I know they are real. I know you are not a witch," he said softly. "Those creatures have appeared in my dreams of late."

Muirne sat up straighter, transfixed by this man who had saved her.

"You've seen these creatures before?" she asked.

"Yes."

"I heard a man say tonight there is another woman, a peasant woman in the village who has had visions of dragons and evil. Surely, this is the evil she dreamt of. I believe it is Freya they speak of."

"I know her," he said, looking into the crackling fire.

Muirne thought of Torvald, knowing he would not let her go so easily, no matter what demons he believed she had conjured.

"I do not want trouble to come to you. He," she stammered, "if Torvald is still alive, he will come for me."

His green eyes darkened, his brow set into a stern expression.

"That man will never get his hands on you. I will make sure of it."

Muirne recoiled into her chair a little. Why this farmer would risk his own life to protect her, a slave he had just met, she could not understand. At the same time, an ethereal energy seemed to be binding her to him. She had never felt this sensation before. Her whole being beckoned her to be still, listen, and hear a message etched in the air around him.

"I believe I have also dreamed of you," he said. She stiffened. "For many weeks, I have had visions, day and night. A golden light appears, a goddess steps out of the light, singing to me such a beautiful melody. These visions came to me before the demons and nightmares. I thought I was losing my mind."

He stopped for a moment. Muirne kept completely still, wondering what this could mean.

"Then tonight, I heard a voice on the wind, and I came to you. Then the demons. I suppose you are my goddess, but I do not know what this means."

A warmth pervaded Muirne's chest once more. The same serenity she felt on the hillside filled her body, telling her this man had purpose, this man was part of her destiny. An otherworldly force drew them toward each other.

He bowed his head again, his shoulders hunched. A sign of distress.

Muirne slipped to her knees before him and took his hands in her own. A bold, brazen gesture, so unlike her. The compulsion to comfort him was too strong to resist.

"I said a prayer tonight when I thought I would perish in the tempest. Something strange happened to me, and then you appeared. I remember feeling—" she stopped, unable to put her thoughts into words.

"Yes? What did you feel?" he asked, lifting his eyes to hers.

She paused, but felt safe to speak of such things to him.

"It was like something didn't want me to go to that circle of stones, as if some other force were trying to protect me from what awaited there. Then my prayers were answered with a heavenly thing that I cannot explain, and you came. You and I," she whispered, voice quivering, "we are bound together somehow. The gods will guide us to our destiny, I am certain. You must trust and have faith. Do not despair, because we have no answers, because danger is upon us. Your dreams tell me we have a part to play against this evil."

Green eyes gazed clear and bright. His frown softened. He smiled, and Muirne's heart leapt again. He was beautiful.

He lifted one hand from hers, brushing his knuckles along her cheek. She did not flinch, knowing this was a kind gesture, not one of ownership. She must learn to trust as well.

"My goddess speaks the truth," he said, pushing back her cascading golden hair. The firelight cast a warm glow on her face. His eyes marked every soft line before peering back into her eyes. "Then we are on this journey together."

AN ANTHOLOGY

Jeremy's Heart

Snow. What on earth was its purpose other than to freeze my ass off? Even in my Wyatt Earp duster, I was freakin' cold, man. Cold.

Ruha beat his drumsticks on a stump next to me. Max sat on another, strumming his guitar. I tapped my fingers on my knees to a different beat. Music consumed us. Sounders heard music all the time—like it streamed through our blood or souls or something, waiting to claw its way out.

My fingers automatically started to play the keys of an invisible piano—Beethoven's "Moonlight Sonata." It was the first song I ever learned. I remembered Ms. Breaux who taught me to play.

I was nine, sitting in my backyard and trying to build a clubhouse out of some rusting tin my dad had piled behind the shed. Seemed like I was always working on some project by myself. Didn't play well with others, as they say. I was doing a piss-poor job of it when I heard music coming from the house next door.

My dad called our neighbor the crazy, old cat lady, so I'd never ventured too close, thinking a witchy woman with a hooked nose and warts hid inside. But that music, so sad and beautiful—it drew me closer. She caught me peeking in her window, but I wasn't scared. She wasn't witchy at all. She had silver hair and smelled like jasmine. Kind of nice, actually.

After filling me up with hot chocolate and lemon cake, she became my best friend. I probably should've been more cautious now that I think about it. She could've been some serial kid-killer or something. But, I knew she wasn't. Even then, I knew the look of loneliness in someone's eyes.

My dad said playing the piano was for pansies, so I never told him that I was sneaking over for lessons every afternoon. I'd sit on the piano bench with a calico curled in my lap then listen, watch, and learn.

I asked her once why she liked Beethoven so much. Never would forget her answer.

"The love of my life played Beethoven for me. I miss him. When I play this music, he comes back to me for a while."

She never told me where he went. I never asked.

Years later when Ms. Breaux's fingers were bent up with arthritis, I'd go over and play "Moonlight Sonata" for her. She'd sit back on her floral sofa, close her eyes, and smile. When she died, I was one of four people at her funeral. She left me her piano, but my dad said we had no room or business with a piano.

The tune wouldn't stop playing in my head today.

"Where is she?" asked Ruha.

"She'll be here soon," I said, snapping back to the present.

As if on cue, Hannah rounded the corner of fir trees. She walked across the clearing where we'd been covertly meeting since our arrival at Mount Haven. I loved to watch her walk.

Damn. Look at her. Long legs, slim hips, white-blonde hair blowing around her perfect face. The surprise was her eyes—dark brown and mesmerizing, like they held a secret.

I wanted to know the secret. I wanted to know everything. If the girl had any clue what she did to me, she'd stop. It should be against the law to creep into a guy's head and invade his thoughts day and night. Still, I kept it casual 'cause I had no idea how to read her. I could never tell if she was being nice or flirty.

Girls confused me. I'd never had a girlfriend before. I almost did, but our time was cut short—too short.

Jessie and I were a perfect fit, despite our different tastes in music. I hated punk. She despised metal. Still, we connected somehow on that freaky night of the football game back in Beau Chêne, Louisiana, when shadow scouts showed up and caused mass hysteria. Jessie gave me a ride home. Except we didn't go home.

We drove to the bayou, sat on the hood of the truck, and talked all night. She dropped me off at my house near dawn. My parents didn't notice, didn't care. I was only worried she would be in trouble.

The last thing she said to me was, "Let's do this again. Say, tonight?"

I agreed. Of course, that night was when Jessie ceased to be Jessie.

The image of the reaper flying into the sky, dragging her with him still haunted me. I couldn't save her. I carried the guilt on my back like Sisyphus pushing his boulder in Hades, day after day.

Hannah stood in front of me now with a sweet smile on her face. The boulder felt a little lighter.

"What's the verdict?" I asked.

"Yes!"

"Alright!" shouted Ruha, hopping up to the news.

Max stopped playing and joined us. Hannah laughed—a throaty, beautiful thing to hear.

"Luke is already setting up in the cafeteria. We'd better hurry if we want to get all of the equipment ready in time."

"What the hell are we waiting for?" I asked. "Let's go."

***

Three hours later, we were ready. We'd covered the windows with black visqueen and set up the stage. I checked the sound system one last time. We were good to go. I couldn't believe it when Roman had slipped me the knowledge that there was a ton of music equipment in the attic above the cafeteria. It took a lot of sneaking around and tuning things up at the old archery field, but we did it. The moment we played for the very first time, it was like we'd been together forever, like fate or something.

I tested the mic when a group of girls opened the door of the cafeteria and crept in slowly.

"Is it true?" one of them asked. "Roman said, he said—"

I glanced at Luke who'd already started thrumming his bass guitar. Ruha drummed a short beat.

"Time to rock-n-roll," I said to Max, looking like he might pee his pants at any minute. "Don't worry. You'll be fine. Just do what we did in practice these past two weeks."

He nodded, his face drained of all color.

The girls at the door squealed in a very girlish way. One took off running back out the door.

Hannah never squealed. Quiet and calm. She reminded me of the Elf Queen Galadriel in *Lord of the Rings*. She actually kind of looked like her, too. Damn.

The whole camp seemed to pile into the room while we finished warming up.

I stepped up to the mic and welcomed the crowd. A pulse of energy hummed in my veins. Usually, my Sounder power stirred only when reapers were near. But, when the Setti gathered in numbers like this, something happened. The room itself came alive.

My clansmen Ben, Mel, and Clara pushed through the crowd toward the front. Clara beamed a smile at me—my sister from another mister. Hannah's eyes were on me. I felt like I might fly when I finally spoke.

"We are Flight of Icarus," I said, as the band started the beat to the first song on our playlist. A line from somewhere, I don't know where, came to mind. "Flying high, trying not to get burned," I mumbled. "This one goes out to the coolest Guardian out there."

We slammed hard into "Firewoman" by *The Cult*. The crowd went insane. The smile on Clara's face was enough. As I belted out the lyrics, my eyes slipped to Hannah, sitting on the edge of the stage, watching me closely. Admiring me? No. Not her. But maybe.

The crowd truly was on fire. Electricity pulsed through the room in rhythm to the music. Setti power vibrated and amplified. Strange that it was invisible, yet so tangible at the same time. When I launched into the opening lines of Nirvana's "Smells Like Teen Spirit," I felt like we could've raised Cobain from the dead with the energy pumping in that room. All the time, Hannah watched quietly from her perch at the edge of the stage.

Above all else, I could feel her energy the most. What's more, I could see it. Her skin began to shimmer white with her Setti power as a Light-bearer.

Her dark eyes caught mine as I screamed the finale of Cobain's tribute to the teens of the world. My heart skipped a beat. The power she wielded with those eyes was unnatural, unfair, and un-freakin'-believable. The song ended. I took a deep breath and held out my hand to her.

"Come on, Lightning, get up here."

She took my hand and jumped to her feet, moving close to the mic. I could hardly breathe when I said, "This one is for all of us."

I stepped back. Luke moved to the piano, leading us into the next tune—the one I'd been waiting for. I stood there and watched Hannah croon the first lines of "Bring Me to Life" by Evanescence.

Beautiful. So beautiful. The girl was going to make me lose my religion. I almost missed my cue when Hannah sang the chorus.

"Wake me up inside!"

I chimed in, echoing her words like Paul McCoy did for Amy Lee. But I didn't see dark-haired Amy Lee. All I could see was her. Hannah, growing brighter with every chord she sang. Her skin glowed from within. I found myself screaming the desperate lyrics and meaning them from the depths of my soul.

"Save me!"

"Save me from the dark," she crooned, gazing at me from deep, brown eyes.

We were close now, sharing the mic. So close I could hardly control myself. Around us, the crowd vibrated with an energy I've never felt before. I didn't see them. I didn't care. My whole being was pulled toward the blonde-haired angel who held my heart in her pretty, little hands.

Then we harmonized, "Bring me to life."

Luke ended the song with the piano melody. The room roared with applause, and I couldn't move. I was frozen. So was she. My eyes fixed on hers. If eyes were truly windows to the soul and if there was ever a time when looks spoke the truth, it was now. I couldn't keep my feelings hidden as I stared at her, while the room was on fire with cheers for more.

She breathed rapidly. Her chest rose and fell at a quickening pace. Finally, I pulled away and took Luke's place behind the piano. This was Hannah's solo.

My fingers found the keys, shaking a little. Hannah dropped her head. Her eyes closed as she began singing "Sally's Song" from *The Nightmare Before Christmas*. She fought for this song to go on the playlist until she won. As she sang the words, I hoped, I prayed they were for me. And I never was the kind of person to do either of those things. For once, I wanted something so far beyond my reach—too good for someone like me.

"Will we ever...end up together?"

How could God create such a creature and plant her in my path? It was torture. My mind reeled. I tried to shake it off, playing the final keys to the song. But it was like a disease. Yeah. I'd been infected by Hannah, and there was no cure. Actually, there was.

I couldn't wait to get through the rest of the songs. I needed to be alone with her. There was no stopping me at this point. I had to know, even if that meant the worst kind of rejection.

I'd lived with rejection all my life—from my parents, my peers, everyone. I'd learned how to cope. Just stop caring. Simple, actually. My Setti clan were the first to embrace me as one of their own. They were the first I let over the wall I'd built. Could fortune possibly smile on me one more time? Or was my world going to come crashing down? I looked at her. God in Heaven, what are you doing to me? I wanted her. Bad.

We ended the night with Stone Sour's "Through Glass," singing about the stars, lies, home and being alone inside your head. Clara had disappeared somewhere, and I never did see Gabe. He'd been his loner self lately. Who knows? Didn't matter. All that mattered was finishing this gig and getting off the stage.

The final eruption of roars and cheers nearly lifted the roof off. Ruha, Luke, and Max came forward. I took Hannah's hand and pulled her to my side. We all took a bow, then another. As people started to crowd the stage, Luke and Ruha stepped up, accepting pats on the back and all that. No way, man.

I gripped Hannah's hand tighter, pulling her with me down the stairs behind the stage. There was a back door by the office. I pushed it open and led her through. It was snowing again. I was only wearing my Iron Maiden T-shirt and jeans. Still, I didn't even feel the cold. How could that be? All I felt was the heat in my veins and the warmth shining off her luminescent skin. She truly looked like an angel, casually leaning back against the wooden building. Watching me pace.

I stopped and turned to stand in front of her. I opened my mouth, but nothing came out.

"Jeremy, the swaggering guy with a cocky answer for everything, is actually speechless."

Damn. The way she talked. Dark eyes drew me closer. I could fall into the abyss and be lost forever.

"What's on your mind, cowboy?"

Funny nickname she'd been using lately. I stepped even closer, so afraid, but in such raw need to touch her. I traced my thumb along her cheekbone, pushing her hair away from her face. She drew in a sharp breath.

"You rock my world, girl," I said, knowing my voice was low and rough.

Her eyes grew a little wider. She was about to pull away, I was sure of it. Then her words stopped my heart from beating.

"And you rock mine," she said, leaning her head toward my touch. "Kiss me. I've waited long enough."

No problem. My lips met hers. Then my body caught on fire. So soft. So warm. I couldn't stop kissing her. She made a whimpering sound. I thought I might be crushing her against the wall, so I pulled her down to the snow. I braced her on top of me, so she wouldn't be cold, never letting her lips part from mine. No way was I letting her go.

I was dreaming. I had to be. Angels didn't dance with devils. They certainly didn't make out with them. Still, she didn't just let me kiss her. She asked for it and kissed me back. With more than a little enthusiasm, I might add.

I rolled over. Her head rested on my arm. The snow melted away from her body. Side effect of a Light-bearer, I guess.

"You really are hot," I said with a grin.

She laughed. God, that laugh.

"There's the Jeremy I know. Making jokes at my expense."

"How is that at your expense? You really are hot—literally and, well, in every other way."

I was aware my eyes wandered, but I couldn't help it. She blushed. I planted several light kisses along one cheek, her eyelids, then back to her mouth. Those lips. Damn. She was melting me from the inside out. I wanted her to be mine. I wanted it so bad I thought I might lose my mind.

I pulled back.

"Why do you call me cowboy?"

She sort of shrugged.

"Come on. Tell me."

She smiled such a sweet smile I wanted to kiss her again. Hell, who was I kidding? I wanted to kiss her nonstop at this point, lock her inside a cabin where no one would bother us for say, eternity.

"Because you are. You're like one of those cool, loner types. And—" she stopped abruptly.

"And what?" I asked, kissing down her jaw to her neck. She paused as I trailed across her windpipe to the other side.

"And sort of lonely like a cowboy."

I stopped and looked at her.

"I'm sorry," she said, "I didn't mean to, well, you asked—"

"No, no," I said. "It's true. I just didn't realize you could see it."

"I don't think everyone can, Jeremy. But I see you, and I like what I see."

I almost came completely unhinged. My hand was in her hair. My lips on her again. I tried not to crush her, but I wanted to get closer, so much closer. I was vaguely aware that her skin began to glow brighter and brighter. When I thought I might make her lips too swollen from my rough need of her, I pulled away. Those half-open dark eyes could've pulled me into Hell, and I would've gladly followed with a stupid smile on my face.

When I finally found my voice, the words that came out weren't exactly romantic.

"You've ruined me."

She frowned.

"How have I ruined you?"

I pulled her hand from my shoulder and pressed it over my heart.

"You feel that?"

She smiled.

"God, girl. You have more power over me than any demonic reaper ever could. I could be cut into a million pieces and never bleed as much as I would with a wound from you."

The danger I was in, dangling my life over the edge of a cliff. I had just opened a door closed too, too long ago—slammed shut and locked tight against the world at large. But now, a gentle hand, a soft voice, a beautiful face lured me to the edge. A bewitching angel peered into that fractured place where a boy played alone. Would she push me over the edge or catch me before I fell?

"Why would I wound you, Jeremy?"

Deep, fathomless eyes. I could drown in the black and die a happy man. I realized then I was shaking. I'd never felt, well, *anything* this much. I'd grown up learning how not to feel a damn thing. It was like my body couldn't take it.

"Jeremy," she said in a soft whisper, "I love you."

She did not just say that to me. Not her. I fell onto my back and closed my eyes. She couldn't love me. I felt her body shift over mine. Her hand swept my hair away from my forehead. I shivered.

"Jeremy? I'm sorry. I know I shouldn't have said that, even if I know it to be true. We haven't known each other that long, but my heart won't deny it. Neither will I."

I opened my eyes to see the dark-eyed angel peering down at me. I cupped her cheek then threaded my fingers into her hair, pulling her closer. I was afraid to say this too loudly. The angels might hear and take her away, back to a safe place far from the likes of me. The door was so wide open, no going back now.

"Hannah, you have enslaved me, heart and soul. It scares the shit out of me, but there it is. I won't love you a little bit or just for a while, I don't know how. I'll love you fully and forever."

My voice came out ragged and uncontrolled. So unlike me. This whole scene was nothing I'd ever imagined. The boy in the dark room wanted something he never dreamed possible.

She smiled.

"Good."

"Good? That's it? I'm your slave forever, and she says good?"

A throaty laugh. Damn, this girl. I wrapped my arms around her and pulled her down to me, promising in my heart to cherish this gift. She planted a gentle kiss on my lips then laid her head on my shoulder.

"Good," she whispered.

"Good," I echoed.

We lay there for I don't know how long. The night remained in shadow around us. No stars, no moon. The reapers had changed the sky into a constant gray slate, blocking out any light from above. Still, I felt no cold with her so close to me.

"What is that you're humming?" she asked after some time.

"What? I was humming?"

"Yes. What is it? Sounds lovely," she said, snuggling closer.

I realized then what tune was in my head.

"It's Beethoven. It's called 'Moonlight Sonata'."

"I love that. Will you play it for me sometime?" she asked softly.

"Of course I will. Whenever you want. I'm your slave, remember?"

She laughed. I pulled her closer, kissing the top of her beautiful, blonde head.

She was my moon in the darkness, lighting my way. The angel loved me, and for once in my Godforsaken life, I finally felt safe.

AN ANTHOLOGY

Fall from Grace

"Come, Sveigja."

I obey, as always. I step over the mutilated remains of Glóð, the *myrkr jotunn* who let the slave girl escape. Bolverk's punishment is swift and final.

Glóð's orders were to keep her close until the making was complete. The girl resisted, finding ways to flee, sealing the doom of her master. She is now in the hands of the Setti. What Bolverk did not know was that I let her go.

I stand before my master, our king. A giant beast with dragon wings and eyes of flame. His bone-blade hangs at his side, smoking from incinerating Glóð into pieces. His other seven-fingered hand comes up and cracks against my jaw. I fall to one knee. The pain is sharp.

"Glóð was under your charge. You too are accountable."

I have never been reprimanded in this manner. I reign in my rage, burying it for another day.

"You are fortunate, Sveigja. Your powers are still of use to me. Or you would be a pile of ash."

A hoard of ash-eaters shriek in the mist, always hovering, waiting for a meal.

"Yes, my lord."

"You destroyed the Setti camp, yet you brought back no prisoners. I have commanded you to bring me a Guardian."

"Yes, my lord."

"You have one in your sight, do you not?"

The Golden One.

"I do, my lord. She is weakening."

"Then bend her. You know what makes them bend, Sveigja. We need the Guardian."

I nod. I will make her bend, but she will not be Bolverk's slave. Never his.

"Go. Do what you must. Report back to me."

I bow and leave. There will soon be a time when I will no longer bow to this king—when I have my queen in hand.

I sift through air and wind, never feeling the elements. A benefit of being a shade. Time slips slowly for us. We move fast, but this world does not. Humans are still scattered, cowering in their homes and wondering who will save them. All the while, we invade and annihilate, city by city.

I slow and stand atop a great building in the vast city, our next target. This place is unlike anything I have ever known. There was no such place when I lived here before in my home world. There is no such place in my new world.

I can feel them. Humans lurking in the buildings below. Behind closed doors. They move swiftly in the daylight. They move not at all in the dark. They know something is near. Something is coming.

My soldiers watch from every alley, corner, and rooftop. Watching from the shadows. Only one can see beyond our shadow cloaks, a Setti Guardian.

Though little light penetrates the constant cloud cover, the world grows darker. I see them. I see her, the Golden One. The male Guardian takes her hand, leads her away from the others to the far side of a metal building. I move in closer, cloaking myself to the highest degree. My Setti power combines with my shadow power to shield beyond the ability of other shades.

I must find a way to bend her will. The boy speaks.

"Just making sure. Jeremy said there were like six of those guys. You're not hurt at all?"

The Golden One, Clara, speaks.

"I'm fine, Michael. Really."

"Yes, you are fine."

He touches her face. He kisses her.

I do not feel emotions as I did when I was human. They are rare and fleeting. I feel anger toward my king, but I hide it well. I feel pleasure when I feed on energy as it courses through my body.

I watch the two Guardians together. Something burns in my chest. This is not anger. This is not pleasure.

The Golden One moves away from him. He whispers. I cannot hear. I edge closer. She turns and looks past him in my direction. She cannot see me, but she can feel me. A good sign. She is powerful, just as I thought. She will be of great use to me.

"What is it?" the male Guardian asks.

"Nothing."

One of the Setti calls the boy's name from around the building.

"I'm coming!"

He moves away ahead of her and speaks again.

"Let's go, Clara."

She nods and follows behind him. When I move directly in the alley where they stood a moment before, she pauses and turns. The boy is gone. I reveal myself to her.

No shock or fear marks her face. She stands in a defiant posture before me, pulling a slender sword from its sheath at her hip.

"What do you want from me?" she asks.

"We have had this conversation once before. Remember? In Mount Haven?"

"Yes, I remember," she responds, her face cold. "You killed many of my friends, and one very dear to me in the fire. I remember."

"That is of no consequence, Guardian. I warned you then that you would regret your decision. Are you ready to make the correct decision now?"

She makes a strange noise in her throat then speaks in a harsh tone.

"Do you mean, have I decided to go with you as you requested and join your demon army? Hell no!"

"I am no demon, Guardian."

"You sure look like one."

Her accusation gives me pause. True—my skin is blackened and tarnished from my transformation. My heart and soul have been long detached from the creature I am now. With every feeding of power from my dark master, humanity slowly fades. I am not the man I was before. I am . . . changed.

"That may be, but the truth is that I long for a different reality than what exists for me at present. A greater one."

"I don't care what you want. I won't go with you, and I know that you can't force a Setti. They must choose. You made the mistake of letting that piece of information slip when we were on that rooftop. Remember?"

I held her in my clutches that night. I could have broken her neck and been done with her. But I did not. Some other power stayed my hand. Now, I chase her, demanding her obedience. She must understand there is no other choice.

I step closer. Her eyes widen. Her sword arm slices toward me. I move very fast, sifting behind her. I enfold her, pinning her arms to her side. She curses and struggles.

"Quiet now, Guardian, and listen."

She stops struggling. Her breathing is fast and unsteady. My Setti power as Vanquisher tunes in to her emotions. I can feel the fear rolling off of her body. I whisper close to her ear.

"I understand your concern for your brethren. This is a noble gesture."

"What would you know about being noble?"

"More than you might realize, little Setti."

"Let me go."

She struggles again. I squeeze her tighter. She stops.

"If you would come with me, all would be right again. We could use our Setti powers together and overthrow the dark king. We could save everyone and leave this world in peace."

"If this happened, who would become king afterward?"

Her emotions swirl—fear, anger, grief, longing. This puzzles me. Her body relaxes when she speaks.

"I would," I tell her in truth.

"And you would be different than the first? You would no longer feed on humans and kill them like cattle?"

"There would be no need, Guardian. You have discovered another way for us to feed, have you not?"

I know what she did to the slave girl. The Golden One turns her head to look at me over her shoulder. I loosen my grip. She understands.

"So you would leave this world in peace?"

She does not fully understand. I clarify.

"*We* would leave this world in peace and go home to our own."

"This is my home. Earth."

I hear her heart beating faster. I feel panic building in her body. I have not used one aspect of my Setti power since I was human. I use it now. I push my own feelings into her—a calm, cold serenity. She slackens in my arms.

"To rule, I need you by my side, Golden One. I need your power *and* mine," I whisper low and clear.

I coat her in a numbing sensation. Her head falls back onto my bare chest. Her hair is soft on my skin.

"You called me that before. Why do you call me that name?"

I do not answer. I have none.

"And what of my friends?" she asks, heavy in my arms.

"I would spare them of any harm."

"No, I mean how could I leave my friends? They are my family, my everything. I couldn't live without them."

"You would not need them anymore."

The wind blows her hair. It brushes my face. Something stirs in me, a sensation long forgotten.

"If I did go, which I won't, what would I become back in your hellish world?"

I sense her fear rising like a cloud. She awakens from the sleepy state I have put her in. I know my answer will incite new terror, but I answer truthfully.

"You would be my queen."

Her breathing increases. I feel the fear consuming her despite the moment of stillness before.

"Clara!"

The male Guardian calls to her from nearby. I hear his steps. The Golden One slips out of my grasp and cuts the air above my head. I lean back, but not enough. She slashes a stinging cut across my face. I growl, feeling the familiar burn of anger from within. She points her sword, daring me to come. I want to punish her. I will punish her.

"I'll never be your queen," she hisses with venom in her voice.

The boy is in sight, eyes wide in horror.

"We shall see," I say, sifting into shadow.

I land on a rooftop not too far away, watching the boy comfort her. I think of the one who once cared for me in this way, the one Bolverk would have killed had I not bended before him. The idea galls me now. I sold my soul for a woman whose face I can no longer remember. Too long in the dark. Faces fade. Names mean nothing. Not so to the humans. To Clara.

I touch my fingers to the stinging welt on my jaw. I watch the boy pull her close in his arms. He cradles her face in one hand. A low growl rumbles in my chest. She will need more coercion to follow my plan. She leans toward him. She looks at him in a way I recognize from a long, long time ago.

I know how to make her bend now.

ABOUT THE AUTHOR

Stephanie Judice is an author of paranormal YA fiction. She calls lush, moss-laden New Iberia, Louisiana, home where the landscape curls into her imagination, creating mystical settings for her stories. She shares her small, southern lifestyle with her husband and four children. As a high school teacher of English and Fine Arts, she is immersed in mythology, legends, and art that serve as constant inspiration for her writings. Some of her favorite things are autumn leaves, dark chocolate, Gothic architecture, Renaissance festivals, family movie nights, and, of course, William Shakespeare. Writing is her haven for self-expression where imagination rules and dreams do come true.

Buy *Saga of the Setti* books on Amazon and Barnes and Noble.

Learn more about Stephanie and her books at:
http://stephaniejudice.blogspot.com
Follow Stephanie on Twitter @sagaofthesetti
Like Stephanie at Saga of the Setti FaceBook and Goodreads

AN ANTHOLOGY

FATE

Annabelle's Story Parting Words

Leigh Michael

Annabelle Walsh thought she had it all. She was living every girl's dream — until her life was turned upside down. All starting with finding out that she's not just a human, but also a water spirit. Half-human, half-sprite to be exact. Although not just any sprite, Annabelle is prophesied to be the only one who can save both the sprites and mankind.

Annabelle's Story is a two-part tale that chronicles Annabelle's mission to fulfill her fate. Through Annabelle's first person prose, we're given an inside look into her fears, her hesitations, her disbeliefs, her courage, her hopes, and ultimately her dreams.

But what about the other characters that bring Annabelle's Story to life? Each character whose destiny becomes a reality upon setting eyes on Annabelle? *Fate* retells this beloved story through the thoughts of Adrian, Aurelia, Blake, and Lady Katherine. These are their parting words.

I know I don't stand alone when I say that cancer has reared its ugly head in my life, affecting those I love. What gives me comfort is knowing I also don't stand alone in the fight against it. Thank you for your purchase of Furthermore and for your part in furthering more cancer research.

Fate is dedicated to all those who take a stand.

ADRIAN

I didn't think it possible, but somehow my love for her deepened. Just the sight of her sent my hand flying to cover my bare chest. Right over my pounding heart. I'd waited so long for this.

Her hair billowed around her, mimicking the movements of the ocean's currents surrounding us.

She is just as I pictured, I thought to myself. *She's more than they said she'd be.*

These thoughts swarmed through my head without yet laying eyes on her face.

She waited with her back to me. Both her arms and legs still, drifting below the water's surface inside a fisherman's net.

I had so much to explain to her. For starters: bad guys, Trackers; good guys, Guardians. Then there was the prophecy that involved her and the different types of water sprites. I hoped the presence of merfolk, encantado, selkie, and fae didn't send her into a tailspin. Or the fact that she wasn't entirely human.

Dismayed, my eyelids closed while my head slowly rocked. I did so not just from the task in front of me, but because I couldn't believe Clemente captured her in such a fashion. First abducting her from her home. Now restraining her within a net. As a Guardian, his job had included bringing her from land to water. It was his job to protect her from the Trackers. She was the "Second Alpha." The one prophesized to retrieve Triton's lost shell and return the power to us; to me as the Prince of Tritonis. But trapping her within a net wasn't quite what I had in mind.

Blinking my eyes open, I stared at her again. Her head circled up, down, and side to side. I couldn't fathom the thoughts that danced through her mind. Hell, she just drowned. Only a few heartbeats ago she realized that she could breathe both water and air.

A mixture of my own feelings swarmed me. My heart thumped, realizing I'd finally talk to her. But a fear also existed to get her to safety as quickly as possible. For all I knew, the Trackers could be lurking nearby.

Without further delay, I uttered her name for the first time.

"Annabelle."

I couldn't help the grin that stretched across my face as her body jumped. Her arms and legs shot out in all directions as far as the net allowed. Like a caged animal, she twisted her body toward me.

Quickly, I replaced my smile with a soft expression. I raised my palms in an effort to bring her ease. In that moment, I'd have given anything to read her thoughts. To get a glimpse into her head. I yearned to know what she thought of me. If she feared me. If she accepted what I was.

However, I didn't need to be a mind reader to spot the confusion in her piercing blue eyes.

They darted across my face. The moment her eyes fluttered over my own, I knew it. It only took that fleeting glance to know this girl was meant to be mine.

The words almost escaped before I stopped them. I forced myself to steady my lips, waiting to speak until I gave her a minute more to understand that I wasn't human.

I imagined her own bottom lip remained in place only from her bite. Then, her eyebrows rose as her gaze drifted lower. My cheeks involuntarily flushed against my fair skin as her brows furrowed.

The confusion in her eyes now mixed with disbelief. She stared at the spot where two legs should've been. Instead, only my two fins. Self-consciously, I stilled them. She knew I was a merman.

I took this as my cue. I wanted to assure her I wouldn't hurt her. Or to let her know it was okay to be scared. Instead something less eloquent came out. "I know this is a lot to handle at once, but we need to hurry."

"Who are you? What's going on?"

"My name is Adrian." I slowly lowered my hands from their outstretched position, resting each against a fin. "I don't have time to explain right now. We just need to get you out of here before the Trackers find us. I don't think they were far behind you."

Instantly, Annabelle's head bolted behind her. As she whipped her head back, her words spilled out, "What are those?"

My body tensed. I tried to keep my voice even, but it was of no use. "The Trackers."

I didn't realize they were that close.

"And what are you?"

"I'm a Guardian and I really need to get you out of here."

Her eyes studied me, making sense of each word. I ached for the next moment to play out differently, but I knew I had no choice. Without further delay, I darted toward her and took hold of the net. With a tug, I pulled her further from the shore. My actions must've caught her off guard. At first, her limp body did nothing to stop me. Then, she turned into a caged animal once more.

While I struggled to maintain my grip on the net, my head bobbed to follow her movements in an attempt to align with her line of sight. "I need you to stop. I'm trying to help you."

"What?" she said, her arms and legs slowing. "This can't be real."

My eyes locked on hers, momentarily losing myself in the hues of blue. "It's very real and very dangerous. You need to trust me."

I paused, waiting for any type of recognition, but she offered me nothing. Exhaling, I tightened my hold on the net and kicked my fins to jumpstart my momentum. This time, she didn't try to stop me.

It didn't take long before my awkward position caused my muscles to burn. Both hands coiled through a hole in the netting, hauling Annabelle behind me as I fluttered each fin in an attempt not to kick her.

Just get her to safety, I prayed. It was all that mattered. The strain in my forearms and abdomen paled in comparison to losing her to the Trackers.

The fear drove me forward. I timed my breathing with the rhythmic motion of my body. My movements smoothed and our speed slowly picked up. Still, I didn't dare look back at her or the Trackers that pursued us. Doing so would only break my concentration.

To my surprise, this concentration and my forward motion would be shattered just seconds later. The selkie's big brown eyes bore into mine as I whipped my head back. His teeth had latched firmly onto the other side of the net. With his thick muscles and seal-like shape, he jerked his body in an attempt to pull Annabelle away.

Although years of hand-to-hand combat and training left my skin weathered, the coarse rope dug into my fingers. Annabelle rocked toward me as I grunted. Then, her attention shifted toward the Tracker who pulled from the other side. Back and forth, her head snapped.

Each time she looked away, my grip slipped further. I tried to kick my fins to generate more momentum, but the selkie likewise flipped his tail. I grimaced as his massive size inched her away from me.

I suddenly flew backward, only catching a glimpse of gray before I met the sandy floor of the sea. The impact ripped the breath from my lungs, but I quickly inhaled. Just as fast, I launched myself back into the fray. Out of the corner of my eye, I spotted Clemente--the gray that barreled into the side of my opponent. The selkie was big, but Clemente was an encantado. His dolphin-like shape dominated the selkie's.

When I wrapped my battered hand once more through the netting, Annabelle leaned away. Her expression hadn't changed. Confusion and disbelief still haunted the soft features of her face, making my heart ache. With each stroke, I fought to push both the water and these thoughts aside.

Thankfully, Clemente had a plan. Annabelle's gasp pulled my attention behind us. There, Clemente and his fellow encantado swam in a tight circle. With a steady whip of their tails against the ocean floor, a circle of sand created an impenetrable wall, trapping the selkie and the other Trackers.

My spirits lifted, I grabbed a broken shell and thrust it toward Annabelle. "Try to cut through the ropes."

She reached out with a shaking hand to take it. The look on her face once again left me pained. What did I expect though? For her to accept me? this? everything?

My frustration fueled each powerful stroke of my free arm. In my other, the jarring vibrations of the net thinning crept up my arm. Her weight shifted as a hole formed.

Without a word, I reached back and pulled the net from her body, avoiding contact with her eyes. I couldn't bear to see the speculation there. I focused instead on the cotton jacket and pants that weighed her down. Once I freed her, I turned away. Now with two arms and full use of my tailfins, I cut smoothly through the water.

Within a few strokes, I realized Annabelle wasn't at my side. I flipped my body to face her. This time I couldn't help but drown in her beauty along with her trepidation and unease. She hovered in the water, her head all that moved. Like when I first set my eyes on her, her gaze darted in all directions.

"Come on!" I said, in hopes of disrupting the deliberation inside her head.

Slowly, she closed her eyes. With her arms pressed firmly against her sides, she ever so slightly nodded her head three times. In an instant, her eyelids flew open to once again reveal the bright blue of her irises. But more than stunning color lingered in her eyes. I couldn't be sure if I caught a glimpse of determination or acceptance. Whatever it was, I let my breath rush from my lungs.

She hesitated only a moment longer before she kicked toward me. Each movement allowed me to breathe easier. I knew the sand barrier surrounding the Trackers served only as a temporary solution.

As I watched her swim, a small smile cracked my lips. With every awkward stroke of her arms and legs, my grin widened. I knew Annabelle swam. Like on a swim team. In fact, she was the star of her team, but my head cocked to the side at the sight of her. Every few strokes, she switched to a different technique.

Just then, her head popped up in my direction, her stare zeroing in on my fins. I quickly dove backward then rotated my body, keeping both my fins together as I accelerated forward. I hoped she hadn't caught my amusement at her clumsy methods of swimming.

"Slow down!" Frustration clung to her voice. "I can't keep up."

Along with curtailing my movements, I waved my arm. "Almost there, Annabelle. Just a little further."

Her movements smoothed as she closed the distance. Although, the intensity in her eyes roughened with each stroke.

"How do you know my name?" she demanded.

"I just do. Now, come on."

She quickened her pace, stopping mere inches from my face. Annabelle's closeness threatened to steal the remaining breath from my lungs as she spoke. "Look, if you don't answer me, I'm not going any further."

"I'll explain later. Right now, we need to keep moving."

"No, tell me now."

I flipped backward, another attempt to hide a grin. I knew she meant to be tough, but she didn't sell it. Not one bit. I called over my shoulder to her, "It's not the time. I need to make sure you're safe. I promise that all your questions will be answered."

When I didn't hear a response, I peeked behind me again. She hovered in the water, rubbing her hands across her face.

Damn, she's cute.

She abruptly dropped her hands. "Fine. Where are we going?"

"To Tritonis. We'll be safe there, and we can figure out our next steps."

I swam forward a few more strokes then stopped as I spotted the glistening current that shot across the murky water. "Right in front of us is a jet stream. It's basically a strong current that runs through the water. Just roll into it and it'll sweep you up. It's easy. Follow my lead, okay?"

She eyed me warily. "I guess so."

"All right, good. Oh, and another thing, we're going to be in there for a while. So feel free to get some sleep if you want. I'll keep watch."

This time, her jaw dropped. A chuckle slipped from my lips. I'd enjoy each new experience with this girl.

I'd been using jet streams ever since I was a boy. Actually, I couldn't remember a time when I didn't use them. They're the fastest way to cross a large body of water. More or less, a tube of accelerated water that stretches across the ocean.

From our location in New Jersey, I calculated we'd reach the northern waters of Africa in just about nine hours. To be honest, I had no idea how long it'd take to swim this distance otherwise. I'd never had a reason to try.

I stole one last look at Annabelle before I over exaggerated my entrance into the jet stream. I acted like a log, rotating again and again until the current swept me up. This motion had become second nature to me. As soon as the jet stream pulled on me, I tightened my core and lengthened my body. A stiff, controlled approach.

I held my gaze on the wall of the jet stream, moving backward within the current. Instinctively my arms shot forward at the sudden appearance of Annabelle. But she held too much momentum. She wobbled for a moment then spiraled out of control. Right out of the other side of the jet stream.

My eyes went wide at her sudden disappearance. I threw my arms and fins out to slow my own momentum. I fought the current with every ounce of strength I had. My body leaned into it, my arms waved backward, and I kicked with both my tailfins held tightly together.

Suddenly, Annabelle popped back into the jet stream. More importantly, she stayed inside this time. At the sight of her, I released my strained muscles. The current took my body like a rag doll, throwing me forward within the water.

I let it take me, relaxing my body and mind. Slowly, I shook my head and exhaled. *This girl is something else*, I thought.

I nonchalantly rotated to steal another glance at her. The jet stream slicked back her light brown hair. Each strand trailed over her lean body, revealing a milky face. A face with wide eyes that took in as much of her current surroundings as possible.

I remembered the way the Elders spoke of her, of her kindness, intelligence, and grace. They tasked Clemente with watching her. Not in a creepy way, but to decipher if she was indeed the "Second Alpha."

Annabelle originally catapulted herself onto our radar because of her swimming skills. A sign of a developing affinity for water. Her local newspaper plastered her name in headlines following every swim meet. It was impossible not to notice her. After two years of careful consideration, Clemente knew without a doubt that she was more than human.

As an encantado he spoke through clicking and high-pitched noises, much like a dolphin. It was something I learned to translate as a young boy. I could still hear the intensity of these sounds as he proclaimed Annabelle to be "the one."

The Elders' excitement had matched my own. But I also felt something else: jealousy. Jealousy that Clemente could shift into a man and venture away from the sea to guard Annabelle. As a merman, my home was here and only here.

I shook the memory from my head. Now Annabelle was here as well. I'd yearned for this moment for the past three years. Actually, for longer.

Casually, I peered backward once more in her direction. My brows immediately lifted. Anxiety pulsed into my body at the sight of her hand testing the limits of the jet stream wall. Her face held a faraway look—one that transformed into panic as her arm shot through the jet stream, nearly pulling her body with it.

"Annabelle!" *Holy shit.* "You can't draw attention to us right now. If anyone was outside the jet stream, they'd be able to pinpoint where we are."

Her eyes didn't quite meet mine as she responded. "Sorry."

"Try to make yourself as straight as possible. You'll go faster and you can catch up." My next words came out under my breath. "That way I can keep a better eye on you."

Moments later, she pulled up beside me, her arm casually brushing against mine.

"Happy?" she said. A hint of bitterness spilled from her voice.

I smiled. "Very."

It only lasted a heartbeat, but I could've sworn something passed over her face as her eyes fell on mine. She quickly hid her expression, but that glimmer taunted me all the same. She had looked... intrigued. Perhaps even slightly enchanted.

It gave me hope that my feelings for her weren't completely in vain.

I chanced another look. This time, she fought with her eyelids to remain open. As she drifted into sleep, my mind drifted from our surroundings, to what lay ahead, and eventually into a distant memory.

"Time for bed, my little prince and princess."

Aurelia chuckled at our mom's words. "Do you think all little girl's mamas call them princesses?"

"I sure hope so, even if you weren't a princess, you'd be mine," she said while lifting my little sister into bed next to me.

Aurelia immediately stuck her tongue out at me and snuggled into my covers. Before I could react, Mom shot me a look. I sighed. I'd only let her stay for story time, and then she had to sleep in her own bed. I was nearly eight years old.

"What story would you like to hear tonight?" my mom asked, eyeing us both.

Aurelia's face lit up. "The profsy!"

She smiled, the corners of my mom's mouth nearly reaching her eyes. I knew this was her favorite time of the day.

"Ah, the great tale of the ABA Prophecy. Great choice my golden dove," she said.

The three of us snuggled tightly in my bed, Aurelia in the middle, as per usual. She was such a baby mer.

Before her words filled the room, my mom reached behind Aurelia and around my shoulder. She caught my eye, and then took a deep breath. "Long, long ago the Titan Gods ruled the world. It was a time of simple happiness. But then… came the Olympians. Zeus punished any men who disobeyed him. He'd take their lives, turning them into evil spirits beneath the earth and evil mers in our sea."

"Mal-vent, right Mama?" Aurelia asked.

"Yes, you're right. They were malevolent."

Aurelia looked up at me with pride, relishing our mom's praise. Suddenly, my chessboard across the room looked like the coolest thing in the world. My mom gently squeezed my arm, pulling my attention toward her.

At our exchange, Aurelia shifted her gaze to our mom then back to me. This time I offered my little sister a ghost of a smile.

Satisfied that I'd behaved as an older brother should, my mom continued, "Soon after, our great leader Triton came into power. He was a fair and just merman who sought to control the evil mers from hurting one another and even humans.

"Adrianus, do you know how he did so?"

"With a conch shell. The currents from it would toss away mers who attacked ships and whip them away if they were being mean to humans on land," I said, acting out each movement dramatically with my free arm.

Mom nodded, then lowered her voice, "But then, his shell was stolen. The thief became known as the 'First Alpha.' Do either of you remember why he was given this name?"

My voice quickly filled the water before Aurelia's could. "It represents the first letter 'A' of the ABA Prophecy."

"Mmhmm. By doing so, he changed things. Triton's shell no longer controlled the evil mers, selkies, and encantado. It became known as the first 'new beginning' just like how the letter 'A' is the start of the alphabet. Sadly, this 'new beginning' also brought pain and destruction. With no one in control, sprites fought each other and humans. Over time, it has worsened."

Aurelia's body rocked into mine as my mom took a deep breath. This time when she spoke, her voice resonated hope, getting louder with each proclamation. "Although we must have faith in the ABA Prophecy because it hasn't yet been fulfilled. One day a half-human, half-sprite boy will be born who possesses all the great affinities of our kind. Like Zeus, he will control the wind. Like Poseidon, he will have power over the water. Like Hades, he will maintain dominion over fire.

And like Arethusa, he will have a connection with earth's energy. He will save us and create a second 'new beginning.' He will return Triton's shell to us. He will allow us to put a leash on the malevolent sprites… on the Trackers. He will be the beta alpha, the 'Second Alpha,' the 'BA' portion of the ABA Prophecy."

My favorite part of the story happened next. Aurelia and I had both heard it many times, but I never tired of hearing about his adventure.

"The prophecy says Triton's shell can only be retrieved from the place the 'First Alpha' hid it—in the deep depths of the Lake of Elfin. But as you both know, no one has entered this mysterious fairy world for thousands and thousands of years. In fact, no one can pass through their trapdoor until an offering has been made. An offering of the same flower that the 'First Alpha' stole from the midst of the lake, ultimately breaking the magical spell that sealed the entrance shut.

"To find this flower, only he can retrieve Arethusa's long lost coins. For you see, they sit in a sunken chest off the coast of the enchanting Graciosa Island. A chest that can only be opened by his hand. It is on these coins that the flower will be revealed.

"But, my children," my mom said, tapping us each on the nose. "The prophecy warns us that this won't be an easy journey for our 'Second Alpha.' Obstacles will haunt him each step of the way. His mind, body, and soul will be put to the test. He will have to dig deep down inside to find strength he never knew existed. Once he does, once he is victorious, he will proudly hold Triton's shell to his lips and release his breath inside. The Trackers will be forced to obey. It will be like a giant net sweeps down from the heavens and rips the evil water sprites away."

Every time I heard of the bravery, strength, and courage of the "Second Alpha" I wished for it to be me. Every time I expressed this to my mother, she'd stroke my hair and remind me how I wasn't destined for this role. Tonight, she had a new response.

"You may not be the 'Second Alpha' my young prince, but you're coming of age. Tomorrow, your training will commence. Should the 'Second Alpha' come during your lifetime, the Elders may select you as a Guardian to protect him as he completes his mission."

"What about me, Mama? Can I be a Guardian too?" my sister asked.

My mom kissed Aurelia's temple before answering. "No, my dear. Our Guardians can only be male, but I believe something big awaits you in your future as well."

Apparently, my sister dismissed the second half of my mom's sentence, focusing solely on the first part. "How come it's always a boy? Why can't Guardians be girls? Why can't the 'Second Alpha' be a girl? It's not fair."

This time, my mom laughed. "Now that I think about it, the prophecy says nothing about the 'Second Alpha' being a boy or a girl. Perhaps she will be female."

Aurelia's eyes lit up, but before either of us could respond, my mom brought our bedtime story to a close. She always did it the same way. Each night, her words circled me in comfort.

"Now it's time for bed my sweet children. As you close your eyes and open them in the morn, always remember three things: faith, hope, love. The faith to continue, hope for what's to come, and love for one another. But always hold love closest to your heart, as it is the greatest of them all."

The thought of love made me think.

"Ma, if the 'Second Alpha' turns out to be a girl, I'm going to marry her."

A smile cracked my mom's lips. "I pray the 'Second Alpha' will soon come, my darling prince. And if it does indeed turn out to be a girl, my heart tells me she will one day be yours."

In the jet stream, my face replicated the smile I remembered from my mom's face over a decade ago. The "Second Alpha" had indeed turned out to be a girl and this was my chance to be with her.

Although for now, the time had come for her journey to begin. For our journey to begin.

Excitement and anxiety fueled my movements as I reached out to shake Annabelle awake. We'd reached Tritonis.

"Perhaps the hardest thing to accept about one's fate, is that it can take years to unfold. But when it does, it's worth every second, every breath, and every dream."

- Adrian

Aurelia

I was four years old the first time I faced heartache.

I mean, *real* heartache. Not, "Mama, Adrian is being mean to me."

More like, "Mama, they ripped Adrian away from me."

Ten years had passed since I uttered those words once barely audible in the midst of my sobs.

The events that lead up to this proclamation happened so fast. In the blink of an eye.

We'd spent the morning journeying home after a visit to another colony of merfolk, the Mami Wata, when the Trackers came out of nowhere.

My family never ventured into the open sea without a fleet of Guardians for protection. Safeguarding the royal family held great importance. That day hadn't been any different. Guardians swam beside Adrian and me, above us, below us, everywhere. What made it different… having them there wasn't enough. The sheer number of Trackers darkened the water.

Instantly, Adrian's fingers interlaced with mine like we'd been fused together. So much so that the sensation continued even after the Tracker broke Adrian's grasp. With one strong hand on my arm and another that threatened to crack the bones in my shoulder, the Tracker tore me from my brother. The momentum whirled me around, time slowing as my gaze caught Adrian's face.

In that moment, the flash of Adrian's eyes on mine catapulted my fear to a level that was completely new to me at my young age. The panic, terror, and regret I saw there fueled the shriek that left my lungs. Instinctively, I called for my dad.

With each stroke the Tracker took to haul me away, my voice raised an octave. My arms and tailfins reached toward my brother as a Guardian whisked him to safety, his body disappearing behind our protectors lined shoulder to shoulder.

The scene that unfolded in front of me couldn't be described as a war. Not even a battle or skirmish. What I witnessed was completely one-sided. Outnumbered by the Trackers, one Guardian fell limp in the water, followed by two more.

The wall of Guardian bodies that once protected my brother cracked, revealing a glimpse of my mom and dad. My eyes immediately locked on my mom's. Between us passed so many emotions. None of which could be described with words. The only thing that left my lips disguised itself as a blood-curdling scream. The Tracker who held me instantly threw his hand across my mouth, muffling the animal-like sound that called to my parents for help.

Upon hearing me, my mom looked deranged. Her arms frantically grabbed onto the shoulders of the Guardians who separated her from the Trackers, but also from me. Just as frantically, the Guardians reacted to keep her safe behind their backs. I remembered seeing my father reach for her, but his hand closed around nothing but air bubbles. My mom had already broken through the thick arms of her protectors.

My hysteria grew with each stroke my mom made toward me. I didn't think it possible, but this hysteria reached a new level when the hilt of the Tracker's sword struck her head and sent her body twisting and turning until she went still.

There were two things I remembered most from this encounter ten years ago. The pain on my brother and dad's face as the Guardians retreated, forcefully dragging them away from my mom and me. And the throbbing sensation that dug deep in my core.

I never wanted to feel that same uncontrollable rise and fall of my chest again. The erratic motion of it caused me to fear for my life, like my lungs would somehow burst. But I would feel it again. Just a few days later my breath labored in my lungs as my mom's life slipped into peril. Actually, her decline happened more like a plunge.

After the sand had settled from the ambush, the Trackers carried my mom's lifeless body and my exhausted four-year-old frame to the dungeons of their underwater colony. I hadn't realized the damage to her head had been so severe, but something inside of her switched off.

There we lay on top of the cold stone floor, my body draped across my mom. Each sob that left my body shook her like a rag doll. When her eyes finally fluttered open, the words flew from my lips and mixed with my tears. "Mama, they ripped Adrian away from me."

I yearned for her voice to sooth me, for her arms to wrap around me and hold me, but her eyes drifted closed once more. For two days she'd awaken to only slip away again. Each time her dark eyes met mine, her whispers raced against the darkness that pulled her back under.

"Golden dove," she said before her head fell to the side.

"My strong girl," I barely deciphered.

"Always remember," she mumbled as I leaned in to catch each word.

The details of those days blurred with each passing year. At one time I could picture every line and crease etched across my mom's face. Now my memory blocked out almost everything from the moment she left me all alone. The only part I allowed myself to remember manifested as her parting words. With her last breaths and ounce of strength, her voice croaked out, "My golden dove, my strong girl, always remember to have the faith to continue, hope for what's to come, and love for another. Love most, my princess."

Then, she was gone.

What happened next became as foggy as my own identity.

"What's her name?" one Tracker had said to another, barely glancing in my direction.

"Does it matter?

"Well, we have to call her something."

"Fine, let's just call her Nysa."

I watched as the first Tracker raised his eyebrow. The second Tracker elaborated, "In Greek, it means goal."

"Um… okay?"

"Well she's the princess of Tritonis. More of a means to an end for us, really. Perhaps we can use her later."

A vindictive smile stretched across his face. "For what?"

"Does it matter? She's not going anywhere. We've got years to figure it out."

Unfortunately, they were right. Days turned into months and into years. Before I knew it, I turned five, then six, seven, eight, nine, and ten.

All the while, I watched and listened. My big blue eyes acted as vacuums for every nook and cranny of their headquarters. Every couple of years, we'd move and rebuild. I'd repeat the process again and again, studying my enemy whenever I could.

It never failed though. At the end of each day, my mom's words passed through my head. Hope, faith, love. The thing was, I never expected to find love here. It seemed impossible in a place shrouded in gray, filled with dark corners, and inhabited with sprites lacking any benevolence. But I did. Not love, love. My heart didn't swell with a crush. I found the type of companionship I once shared with Adrian.

A few days after I turned eleven, the Trackers captured a young mer from a nomad colony. One of my many menial tasks included delivering meals to other prisoners and to the Trackers themselves

I hated giving food to those being held captive. The last time we established a colony, the leader gave me a real room, upstairs. Granted, the stark walls, rotted cot, and single trunk left much to be desired, but it far exceeded being in the dungeons.

Each time I pulled open the heavy doors that led to the cells, my heart sunk. I knew how it felt to be trapped and alone. On this day, I did a double take at the sight of a new prisoner. He had curled his body in such a way that it created a challenge to see his face. He had tucked himself deep into the corner of his cell. His back pressed firmly against the stone wall.

"Hello?" I called to him.

He didn't move, not even a twitch.

I tried again. "I have food for you."

Still nothing. That first day, I spent three minutes trying to coax him from the corner.

The second day, I hovered outside his cell for five.

I couldn't help but feel drawn to him. The hair of most mers took on a dark shade of brown. In fact, I'd never seen anyone's whose didn't... until now. Each strand on this boy's head glistened a golden blond. Just like mine.

Maybe I sought a kinship with him for this reason. Or maybe I so desperately needed to no longer feel alone. I kept going back, reassuring him that I wouldn't hurt him and that he needed to eat. On the fourth day, I grasped the bars and pressed my face as far through the space as possible. "What's your name?"

My grip tightened as his head ever so slightly turned toward me. For the first time, I caught sight of his face. More specifically, his green eyes.

My own blue eyes went wide. Never before had I seen a merman with an emerald hue. Just like brown hair, brown eyes were the norm. I had always felt special due to my uniqueness, especially since my position within the Trackers consisted of servitude. I revered it as a sacred piece of myself.

This boy was special too. As I stared at him, my mind once again drifted to my mom. However, this time, my memory replayed a different set of words.

While coiling a strand of my hair around her finger, my mom had once said, "You know, my dear, others before you have had golden tresses."

"Really?" I had responded, a twinkle in my eye.

"Why, yes. You certainly didn't get your hair and eye color from your father and I. You see, your delicate features are much like Aphrodite, one of your great aunts from long ago."

My heart had swooned thinking that any part of me could've resembled the goddess of beauty.

Chuckling, my mom must've appreciated my awe. "There were others with locks similar to yours."

"Like who?" I had said, miffed that others shared this same comparison to Aphrodite.

"Well, Helen of Troy for one. I believe another was Ganymede."

"Ga-ny-mede," I repeated slowly, sounding out each part of his name. "Was he a god?"

"No, my princess. Ganymede was a mere mortal. One whose beauty caught the eye of Zeus. Our great myths have said that Ganymede tended to his flock of sheep when an eagle swooped down and snatched him."

Her arm cut through the water. I jolted.

"Some say Zeus sent the eagle," she continued. "Others believe Zeus transformed himself to act as this bird. Whatever the case, Zeus wanted this boy for himself and gave him the position of cupbearer to the Gods in Olympus. A role that held great honor."

"He was handsome?"

"Yes, Zeus marveled at his blond hair and bright green eyes."

At the time, the story had acted as a simple way to help my eyes grow heavy before bed.

Now, it seemed ironic.

A boy in the spitting image of Ganymede had been captured once again.

Slowly, his head rose from the stone ground. He eyed me curiously, wiping his long hair from across his face. "Who are you?"

"My name's Aurelia." The Trackers may have referred to me as Nysa, but over the years my resolve strengthened. I was Aurelia, princess of Tritonis.

His gaze inched little by little over me, lingering on the food I had placed by my fins. I watched his stoic face, trying to decipher his thoughts.

"Whatcha got there?" he asked nodding toward his breakfast.

Before I could stop it, a smile cracked my lips. "You're gonna have to tell me your name first."

"Christos."

"Nice to meet you, Christos."

It was one of the first honest things that had left my lips in over seven years.

For the next three years, Christos and I were inseparable. Well, almost. As much as I begged for him to be brought upstairs from the dungeons, Alastor refused me. He ruled the evil sprites, but he didn't fool me. I sensed his weaknesses.

Still, the time Christos spent in the dungeons meant separation by the cold metal bars. I savored the time we spent in the exercise yard. Free to swim and play. Mostly, we devised ways to escape. Soon we'd put our strategy into action. In fact, we'd already taken steps to fulfill our plan.

Before we could make our next move, life decided to alter my path once again. In the middle of the night, a Tracker burst into my room. I quickly shot up in my narrow cot as he told me my services were needed.

That was a rarity. Not me serving them, but the fact the corals hadn't yet woke. Beneath the sea, the sleep patterns of the coral created our day and night. Generally, Alastor didn't call upon me until the first coral glimmered.

I quickly swam through the dark halls toward the meeting room, putting into place my subservient façade. As I turned the corner into the final hallway, voices seeped from behind the closed door.

What's going on? I thought.

Pushing the door open, Alastor's rough voice demanded attention from the Trackers in the room. A soft glow from the concealed fire caused his face to look more sinister than normal as he spoke. "Where are the girl and boy?"

The selkie who hovered closest in the water responded through barking sounds. I've been able to translate their voice ever since a young age. "The dungeons, sir."

From where Alastor sat at the head of the table, his gaze dropped to the floor. Meanwhile, I slipped into the shadows against the far wall. I wouldn't say a word until he demanded something from me. I'd enlisted this tactic time and time again, listening whenever I could.

His eyes locked onto a mermaid named Kerberos seated at the table. "Tell me what happened."

"We followed protocol, sir. Stalking the girl and boy until they located the sunken chest. The boy exited from the alcove first with the coins in hand. Collins and I quickly controlled him." The mermaid then nodded toward a selkie. "He banged into the boy and bit at his hands. That's when the girl came out. She's weak and froze in place. By that time, Ryan had stolen the coins and fled.

"What the prophecy says about her is true. She has the powers of the 'Second Alpha.' She released a current at us that knocked the boy free. We quickly recovered control of him but she'd already gone after Ryan. With the boy under Collins' control, I followed. She moved at an incredibly fast speed. I didn't catch her until she'd reached land. Ryan stood on the shore with the coins. I incapacitated her."

While Kerberos spoke, Alastor stared at the wall and stroked his long, dark beard. I also tried to comprehend what this meant. I knew the "Second Alpha" had been identified. I knew the Trackers had pursued her on land and the Guardians had brought her to water. That part provided me with great delight. It seemed she'd found the coins. Problem was, the Trackers now had them.

Alastor's words cut through my thoughts. "Why did you go to land?"

The selkie he addressed cowered under his glare. "I've heard of the girl's powers. I thought it was our best chance to escape with the coins." He glanced toward another selkie, his father—who didn't acknowledge him.

Dismissively, Alastor waved his hand. "Just show me the coins."

A look of greed washed over his face as a mer untied the velvet bag and emptied it onto the table. Dozens of coins lazily spilled out, clamoring against the wood.

His giant hand scooped up a few coins, leaning closer to the flames to illuminate each piece of silver. He held an expression I couldn't quite pinpoint. Moments later, he threw the coins back against the table. There was no mistaking the look of disdain on his face as he did so. His next words came out like venom, and this time he directed them at me. "Nysa, get the Elders. Now!"

Without any hesitation, I left the room. As quickly as I could, I gathered the four mer responsible for aiding Alastor in decisions. A position I'd never want. Each only held the title for a short period of time. Not because the job had a limited duration, but because Alastor disposed of any who advised him on a decision that didn't meet his satisfaction.

The tension in the room made me shiver, but I didn't dare rub my arms. Over the next few hours, the Elders, Alastor, and the Trackers who'd retrieved the coins discussed their next course of action. I listened closely while bringing food, clearing dishes, and completing other thankless tasks. By the time the Trackers had formed a plan, the soft glow from the corals spilled in through the single window. The beam of light hit the center of the table, showcasing the coins, then landed on the dying coals of the fire.

What I felt inside mimicked the fading embers. Their plan caused a piece of me to darken, but I still held a twinge of a spark. I wasn't going to let them destroy my people. It didn't matter that I hadn't set eyes on them in over a decade. They were still mine.

"What're we going to do about the girl and boy now?" the selkie posed.

An encantado answered in his clicking noise, much like a dolphin. "We have no real need for her anymore. The boy never served a purpose."

The brown eyes of the selkie went wide. "We're just going to kill Annabelle?"

"Annabelle? Since when do we call her by name?" Kerberos asked.

"I scouted her. I've always done so."

"Not to us you haven't. But fine, let's just kill *Annabelle*."

Another selkie chimed in. Then another. Back and forth they debated on the fate of the prisoners. I couldn't pinpoint why Ryan so adamantly believed their lives should be spared, but I felt thankful he took this stance. All the while, Ryan's father eyed him with suspicion.

I snapped to attention when Alastor's voice filled the room. "Enough!"

The sounds of their heated fracas immediately halted. Silence filled the once noisy and disorderly room.

"That's enough," he growled again. "The chest has been opened. She no longer has value. Dispose of the girl."

I exhaled when Ryan didn't say another word. In the past, I'd seen Alastor ruthlessly strike like a sea serpent. I didn't want to witness that again.

Instead, I slowly kicked backward until my hand found the door. In as fluid of a motion as possible, I swung it open and slipped out, soundlessly closing it at my back.

As soon as I turned, I came face to face with a young girl. There was only one person she could be. They had just decided her fate.

Without thinking, I threw her against the wall. My arm pressed firmly against her throat. Leaning closer, I whispered, "Shh, don't say a word."

How did she get up here? I thought.

Annabelle stared blankly back at me. The confusion in her bright blue eyes must've resembled my own. I twisted slightly to peek toward the door. This wasn't good. This wasn't good at all. A roomful of sprites who wanted her dead sat just a few feet away. I raised my free arm to point down the hallway. Her gaze followed my finger obediently as I brought it to my lips. I peered at her until I knew she understood. A slow nod then hurried shake of her head told me she did.

Satisfied, I removed my arm from across her throat and grabbed her hand. Together, we kicked toward the foyer. We only swam about twenty yards or so, but the entire time I held my breath, looking back every few feet to make sure no one else left the room.

Once in the foyer, I exhaled the little breath that lingered in my lungs.

"What are you doing here?" I whispered. "You are lucky they didn't catch you."

A slight sound snapped my attention back toward the corridor, but the hallway still remained empty. My body was on edge. As I glanced back at Annabelle, her arms shook by her side. She clearly felt the same.

"Did you hear me?" I tried again in a hushed voice. "How did you get out of the dungeons?"

She offered me no type of verbal response. I could tell her mind hadn't yet processed the situation. Her mouth twitched as she formed words in her head, but nothing left her lips.

Reassure her, that was what I needed to do. I wasn't one of the bad guys. The words just about left my lips when she finally spoke.

"Aurelia?"

My body rocked backward like a wave hit me. Back and forth my head shook.

How the hell did she know my name? My real name.

The tables had turned. It was me who now needed to be reassured. "What did you just say?"

Her response held no delay this time, each word running into the next. "Your name. It's Aurelia? Right?"

I gasped. "How'd you know that? No one has called me that in years."

Except for Christos, I thought. *Did she meet Christos in the dungeons?*

"Your hair, your age, the shape of your eyes." She paused, looking intently at me. "Adrian."

"That's impossible."

"What is?"

"My brother is dead," I growled. "How dare you talk about him."

"No, no, no. He's not. I swear."

"They told me they killed him after my capture… along with the rest of my family."

Annabelle glanced at the ground, then pointed where she'd just looked. "Aurelia, I, um, Adrian is down in the dungeons."

"What?!" I shrieked.

Adrian is the boy they captured? The one they stole the coins from?

I'd swam from the foyer to the dungeons countless times. Now, my arms and tailfins moved instinctively. As I dove through the hole to the lower level, there wasn't room in my head to decipher my movements, only my thoughts. Faith, hope, and love. When it came to my family, I thought I lost all three of these things long ago.

I violently threw open the first heavy door, not caring if I now made any noise. Quickly looking to the left and right, the first quad of cells remained empty. I dove toward the next door, ignoring Annabelle as she called my name.

After slipping through the doorway, I acknowledged four more empty cells. I darted past them and wrapped my hand around the handle of another door. Tears had already puddled behind my eyes.

The weight of the door strained my arm as I pulled it toward me, nearly losing my grip at the sight of him through the crack that'd formed. His hair was longer, darker. The strong lines of his face still remained. He just looked older, more mature.

There was no stopping the tears now. *My brother*, I thought. *Adrian is alive.*

He didn't see me at first. Something else captivated his thoughts. But as soon as his mind registered the motion to his right, the recognition exploded in his eyes.

"Aurelia!" he gasped and launched himself to the front of his cell.

In a blink, I met him there.

"You're alive," he said, reaching through the bars to drag me closer.

I only nodded. The words not yet ready to come out. Just tears. Lot of tears.

"Ma? Is she here too?"

"No," I whispered, momentarily looking away. Then the words all came pouring out. "She woke, but then grew sicker and sicker. She told me, Adrian. Just like when we were kids. She told me the three words, then she died. I wanted to die too. I wished for it. But I kept hearing those words. I didn't give up. I didn't give up because of Mama."

Adrian's eyes had closed while I spoke, when he opened them a look of protectiveness mixed with his tears. "Did they hurt you? Did the Trackers ever hurt you?"

I shook my head. "I wasn't worth anything to them. Not yet anyway. They hadn't yet figured out a way to use me."

"I'll kill them. They may not have touched you, but they took you away from us."

"From us? Is Daddy alive too?"

"I'm sorry, Ari."

I almost burst upon hearing this nickname again. To have my brother back. I came to terms with losing my father long ago. I needed to focus on the positives and count my blessings that my big brother was here.

"Adrian," Annabelle called, not realizing she hovered behind us. "We need to get out of here. Now!"

"Do you have the key?"

"No, I saw Aurelia and—"

I whipped toward Annabelle. "I know where it is."

"You do? Go get them!" she said.

Adrian grabbed my arm, bringing my attention back to him. "Wait, no. Aurelia, it's not safe."

"Adrian, we're running out of time. We need her help," Annabelle pleaded.

I knew she was right. Before Adrian could respond, I kicked backward to break the hold he had on my arm. Without any hesitation I darted toward the door I'd entered through only a minute ago and back through the two grouping of cells.

I hadn't intended on implementing Christos' and my plan yet, but I knew it was now or never. As soon as I entered the foyer, I paused for a heartbeat. The slight sound of movement above kicked me into action. First I dove to my right, the doorframe on the far side held a small key along the top ledge. It didn't belong to that door though. I'd learned over the years it unlocked the door on the other side of the room. With a few strong kicks of my fins, I grabbed ahold of the other door and threw the key into the lock. Once in the room, my fingers brushed against the rows of keys until I located the right one. My hand also closed around a small device.

I smiled as I hurriedly swam toward my brother and Annabelle. Those stupid Trackers underestimated me. Part two of our plan: accomplished. Part one happened months ago. We'd just been biding our time.

Without saying a word, I drove the key into Adrian's lock and swung the door open. After shoving the device through the neck hole of my tightly woven shirt, I turned to my brother.

"Let's get out of here!" he said, taking hold of my hand. "Which way?"

I simply pointed toward the other door and Adrian kicked toward it, creating a triangle formation as he dragged Annabelle and me behind.

My heart raced as we entered into the next cellblock. With the key ready in hand, I whipped to the right expecting to see Christos, but he wasn't there.

My heart just as quickly plunged.

Adrian didn't notice as he continued to pull us into the next block of cells.

Thoughts bounced around in my head, barely noticing as Adrian yanked me to a stop. Annabelle's high-pitched scream ripped me from my daze, "Natasha! Shamus!"

I followed her voice. In opposite cells a mermaid and selkie clung to the bars. I remembered them from my early years, racing around the lunchroom until Ms. Lazos settled us down. Just like Adrian, they looked more weathered. Their eyes no longer held the innocence that accompanied childhood. I was sure mine didn't either.

The motion of Annabelle's frantic arm gesturing at me pulled me from my self-reflection. "Hurry! Open their cells!"

Annabelle immediately threw her arms around Natasha. The familiarity she had with Natasha startled me. I'd missed so much being here. The Trackers stole my adolescent years from me. I wouldn't let them steal anything else, especially not Christos.

Our group of five darted toward the door and into the next grouping of cells. That was when the slamming of the first door reached our ears. Only five doors now separated us from the Trackers.

"How much further?" Adrian called.

"Just ahead through those doors. There's an exercise yard for prisoners."

We burst through them, leaving the dungeons behind.

The brightness of the corals stung my eyes, but I didn't have a moment to delay. I peered through the pain to find him. My mind quickly registered a handful of imprisoned mers scattered around the open area.

Where was he? He's gotta be here.

I frantically kicked my legs to keep up with my long lost friends, brother, and Annabelle as my head swiveled from side to side.

Then, his blond hair caught my eye.

"Christos!"

His head snapped toward mine, hair momentarily wrapping across his face. "Aurelia!"

"Go," I said. "Get it!"

Adrian's frantic words to go faster faintly reached my ears as I watched Christos dive in the opposite direction.

Part three of our plan was underway. I just feared there wouldn't be enough time.

As our group distanced ourselves from the dungeons, I slowed. Adrian's eyes burned into mine as I drifted behind. "Aurelia, what are you doing?"

I held up my wrist, revealing the tracking bracelet that'd kill me instantly if I crossed the boundaries of the exercise yard. The red light already blinked rapidly.

I needed Christos to return with the second device. The final part of our plan. This device did a few things. It opened the doors back into the dungeons. And when pressed simultaneously to a bracelet with the other device, the bracelet unhinged.

The Trackers each possessed this second one. Months ago, Christos had feigned an injury, engaging a Tracker with his screams. I snuck up behind the Tracker and slipped it from his belt. Since then, the device hid beneath a patch of coral across the yard. The Tracker never reported it missing, fearing the wrath of Alastor. At first, he seemed on edge, but when nothing happened over the next few weeks, I witnessed the Tracker's tension slip away.

Now, tension all but oozed from my brother. With his hands wrapped around the bracelet, he pulled. The metal dug into my wrist but I didn't make a sound. My heart already broke with the groans slipping from Adrian's lips.

My head shot toward the dungeons as the door flew open and two mers came barreling out.

It's too late for me, I thought. *Not for my brother and friends.*

Adrian grabbed my face, forcing me to look at him again. "I won't leave you!"

"Don't be stupid! There's nothing you can do! Get out of here!"

He shook his head, dropping his hand back to the bracelet. All of a sudden, Annabelle pushed him out of the way and threw her hands on it instead. A glimmer in her eyes gave me hope.

"Let me try!" she screamed.

But as she pulled, my tender skin scorched with pain and I cried out. Annabelle jerked her hands away, a look of concern passing over her face. I turned my head back to the approaching Trackers, they were now halfway across the exercise yard, only fifty yards away. I looked beyond them, hoping to see Christos, but he hadn't yet returned.

I tore my attention back to Annabelle and my brother, about to tell them again to leave me, when the words caught in my throat.

Annabelle hovered in front of me, shaking her hands at her side. Tendrils of steam slipped from them and disappeared into the surrounding water. Before I could react, she covered my bracelet with her burning skin. In an instant, the heat seeped into my own. I bit my bottom lip as I endured the pain. Little by little, Annabelle reshaped the bracelet loosening it from around my wrist.

With the last bit of color disappearing from her face, she yanked her hands away and went limp into the water. Adrian caught her and yelled to me, "Ari! Slide your hand out!"

My skin looked red and blistered, but I didn't care. It was the first time in ten years that the heavy metal didn't don my wrist.

"Go!" they screamed in unison. I flipped my tailfins to jumpstart my momentum as Adrian led Annabelle by the hand.

I spared another glance toward the Trackers. The first mer twenty yards away carried a gun. The second trailed slightly but held a gun as well. But that wasn't what sent my heart racing. Christos kicked fiercely behind them.

Hesitation consumed me only a moment longer before Adrian's intensity hit me.

Christos would catch up, I told myself. I needed to keep moving.

The three of us raced to join Shamus and Natasha. They had already crossed the boundary of the exercise yard. Thankfully, the Trackers didn't put bracelets on any of them.

As I approached this same boundary, a thought crossed my mind.

I tore the device from my shirt and carefully released it into the water. I watched as it sank deeper and deeper, hoping the current wouldn't carry it too far.

I really should've been watching for the closest Tracker.

The net he fired hit me and bent me in half. My tailfins slapped my face as it threw me backward.

"Help!" I screamed.

The scowl of the Tracker held my gaze as panic ensued. He was a Tracker I'd become familiar with. Kerberos. Alastor had made a habit of calling upon Kerberos for the dirtiest of deeds. His name derived from the three-headed dog that once guarded the entrance to Hades. I wouldn't let my mind slip into the memory of how he tortured a mer just last week. I didn't want to relive that moment ever again.

His arms and legs moved at such a speed it seemed impossible. Greed and hatred filled his eyes as his outstretched hand closed the distance to me.

I remained helpless within the net, my tailfins awkwardly bent shielding half my face.

Right before his fingers slipped through the net, my body jerked backward. As I twisted my head to the side, Adrian with his hands wrapped through the netting filled my vision.

My mind froze until the memory hit me like a tidal wave. The panic, terror, and regret etched across his face mimicked the same expression from ten years ago.

A jolt came from other side. My head snapped toward Kerberos.

Desperation consumed me as I looked again at my brother. He avoided my eyes as the muscles in his arms shook and his tailfins ferociously kicked within the water.

Like a rag doll in the middle, I got tossed back and forth by whichever mer momentarily held the upper hand.

Please, I thought. *Please don't let me lose Adrian again.*

I closed my eyes and prayed to Tykhe—the goddess of fortune and fate.

An impact sent my eyes flying open. Kerberos no longer held onto the netting. Neither did my brother. Nothing but air bubbles surrounded me.

Not even a second later, a hand cut through the cloudy water, revealing my brother's face.

"It's Clemente!" Annabelle called from outside the air bubbles.

Instantly, I pictured the dolphin-like shape of the encantado, another sprite from my early years. The pieces came together. He'd caused the impact that released me from Kerberos' grasp.

With the air bubbles fading away, I tried to locate Christos in the distance, but I didn't see him anywhere. I feared the worst, that the other Tracker had grabbed him.

Adrian's hand slipped again through the netting, hitting me in the arm as his fingers closed around the coarse rope. It brought my attention back to him. With a tug, he dragged me closer to Clemente and Annabelle.

"Grab onto his dorsal fin!" he called to her.

He then pushed me toward Clemente who secured the netting between his rows of tiny teeth.

As Clemente cut across the water, Adrian latched himself onto Clemente's other side. Moments later, Natasha clung to his body as well.

My mind still lingered on Christos. Without him, I wasn't sure I'd have survived the last three years. But it was the love of my family that got me through the first seven. The thought of being reunited with anyone in my family never seemed possible. Now that it had happened, I didn't want to give that up. I couldn't.

Clemente tossed me from his mouth to Shamus'. I barely acknowledged this transfer, only how the resistance of the water grew. Over the next ten minutes, the distance rapidly increased between the Trackers and us. But also between Christos and me.

I'll come back for you, I silently promised him.

As we fled from the Tracker's town, a sense of accomplishment coursed through my veins. I dreamed of escaping, but doubt always lingered in the back of my mind. Regret now replaced that doubt. I had left Christos.

When we finally came to a stop, I smoothed my hair and pulled my shirt taunt, welcoming the distraction. Adrian appeared in front of me a moment later with a shell in hand. While he worked to cut the net, he faced Annabelle, "Belles, what did you do back there?"

"I'm not really sure, my hands just got so hot."

"Your affinity for fire..." Natasha said. "It developed."

Adrian shook his head from side to side as he cut, never looking up. "You saved Aurelia."

His words washed over me. He was right. She'd saved me. Christos and I may have put a plan in motion months ago, but without Annabelle I may never have gotten out.

I crawled out of the hole Adrian had created in the net and threw my arms around her. "Annabelle, I don't know how I can ever repay you. First helping me find my brother and then giving me my life back."

I meant every word. She didn't respond though, she just stroked my hair until Clemente's clicking sounds pulled us apart. At Annabelle's blank stare, Natasha translated, "He says we need to keep moving, we're not safe here."

Annabelle's eyes scanned our small circle. "Where are we supposed to go?"

In response, my brother scrubbed his hands over his face.

When did he turn into dad? I thought to myself.

"I don't know," he said. "We never got a look at the coins. I don't know where we're supposed to go next."

I smiled internally as I reached inside my shirt. "You mean this coin?"

Five sets of eyes latched onto the silver I held in my hand.

Annabelle spoke first. "What! You can't be serious. How did you get that?"

"You little sneak," Adrian chimed in as he threw his arm around my shoulder.

Pride swelled inside of me. I tried to remain casual. *Cool as a cucumber* as a human would say, but I couldn't hide my excitement as I responded, "Please, I'm just their humble servant. They never take notice of little ol' me. I simply grabbed a coin along with their plates."

"Well, let me see," Adrian said. I handed it to him, watching as he flipped it over. "It's Arethusa."

I nodded. "Yeah, that's what the Trackers said too. Dolphins encircle her."

Annabelle swam closer, leaning over my brother's shoulder. "But I don't see a flower on it?"

She was right. I remembered how my mom told us the coin would reveal the type of flower that acted as an offering at the Lake of Elfin. The only flower that would unlock the trapdoor and allow entrance inside. There, Triton's shell waited to be recovered.

But one side of the coin showed only the profile of Arethusa. Surrounding her face, a circle of dolphins created a layer of protection. Her medusa-like hair was flowerless, the dolphins didn't reveal any flowers, and neither did the rest of the coin.

With a shrug of my shoulders, I answered Annabelle's question. Well, really, I guess it was more of a statement. "That threw the Trackers for a loop as well. Actually they talked about it for hours."

"And?"

"Well, I'm not entirely sure what they figured out. I was sent to fetch more food. But as I left, I heard them say something about the New World Tropics."

"The what?" Annabelle asked.

A flurry of clicking sounds from Clemente provided an answer. This time, Adrian translated for Annabelle, "He says it's the area around the equator, between the Tropic of Cancer and the Tropic of Capricorn. So Central America, South America, Africa, parts of Asia and Australia."

Annabelle said something. I'm not sure what. My mind was too busy scheming. This action had become second nature over the years. "There's gotta be somebody who can help us."

"Aurelia," Adrian said, pulling my attention to him. "You do realize that you aren't coming with us."

"What? That's ridiculous." Now that I was free, I wanted to help them. My mom planted the seed of the prophecy in my mind long ago.

"No, it's not ridiculous. For all these years I thought I'd lost you. There's no way I'm risking your safety any further. Besides, YaYa is going to be thrilled to see you. She thought she was never going to see you again."

My bottom lip dipped open, ruining the tight lips I maintained before in my state of defiance.

The allure of seeing my grandmother caused me to forget about the prophecy. Just half an hour ago, I didn't think I had any family left.

His eyes watched me before turning toward Natasha. "You aren't going to like this either, but I need you to take my sister home. I know YaYa would trust you to make sure she gets there safely. I trust you."

Disappointment flashed across Natasha's face, but her features quickly smoothed. This wasn't the same carefree girl from my childhood. Nothing but focus and determination could be seen in her eyes.

"Go, now," my brother said. "We've already wasted enough time."

He pulled me into a hug before he continued, speaking only to me. "Ari, our quest to fulfill the prophecy would've been over without you. You've given me the faith, hope, and love I needed to keep going."

His words touched me. As Natasha wrapped her arm around me and flipped us in the opposite direction, I twisted for another look at my brother.

I had helped them. Now, I had to help another. Dangling YaYa in front of me worked to sway my thoughts from the prophecy, but now they slipped once again to Christos. He was also my family.

As Natasha and I swam toward the nearest jet stream, I tried to align the right words in my head. The seriousness in her eyes warned me I needed a good defense.

"Natasha, I need to go back."

"Princess Aurelia, that is not an option. They will be okay without us."

"I know that, but Christos won't."

The lines of confusion in her forehead barely formed before her face morphed into that of a warrior's. Another's voice had answered my plea. Before I knew it, her body stood between whoever had spoken and me. I'd never seen a mer move so fast.

"I'll be okay," he repeated.

Excitement surged.

"How did you find us?!" I squealed as I peered around Natasha.

Christos beamed at me. "It was smart of you to drop the other device."

I couldn't be happier. Now, I had both my brothers back.

"The thing about fate is that no one knows what you're meant to be or what you will become. Sometimes you surprise everyone, even yourself."

- Aurelia

AN ANTHOLOGY

Blake

You can do this, I told myself. *You have to do this.*

But I couldn't move from my hiding place behind the shrubs. Annabelle and I had been inseparable for the past year of our lives. Boyfriend and girlfriend. My Belles. It didn't start that way though. As I watched her between the branches, my mind pieced together the first day we'd met. The memory flashed before my eyes with shame.

I'd stepped out of my piece of crap car in the parking lot of our school. In the distance, the leaves were beginning to fade from their deep green hues to announce the coming of autumn. The air warmed me even with the slight breeze.

I didn't mind my time on land in my human form, but I preferred the warmer months. The thought of enduring the colder weather held zero allure. I'd been here for a few weeks and dreaded the upcoming snowfall. But now that we believed the girl to be the "Second Alpha" the time had come to make contact.

Today would be the day. For the past week, I'd seen her eyeing me up as I passed in the hall. She knew who I was. Well, she knew me as the new kid in school—that was the extent of it. The fact I was a selkie or that my true intentions included gaining her trust so I could later drown her didn't even cross her pea-sized brain.

The thought made me smile. Humans were so weak, and especially the female ones. I really hadn't expected the "Second Alpha" to be a girl. It'd make it easier, though, to woo her. Then I'd see if she could breathe water like air. If not, oh well. If she did, then I'd welcome my promotion within the selkie ranks after I hand-delivered her to Alastor.

As I took my first steps across the parking lot, my pace immediately faltered.

What on earth was he doing here?

With my hands fisted, I stomped across the pavement, ignoring the idle classmates who stood in the way. My shoulder brushed against one and I mentally dialed my intensity back. I couldn't be perceived as the jerk in school. With a slight turn of my body, I shot him a nod as a peace offering. I hated playing nice.

Besides, it was my brother who made my blood burn. There he stood, that cocky bastard, talking to a pretty little blonde. The wheels in my head turned in full motion by the time I approached them.

"Sarah?" I asked, pulling her attention to me.

Her face lit up as she followed my voice. "Oh, hi Blake."

I love that my reputation preceded me. Also that I happened to have class with the girl my brother chose to flirt with.

"Sorry to interrupt," I said pleasantly. "I just ran into Mr. Snyder and he asked if I've seen you yet this morning."

Concern passed over her face and she cautiously scanned the parking lot and front of the school. "Did he say why?"

"Nah, he didn't."

"I guess I should go find him," she said before plastering a smile back onto her face. "It was really nice meeting you, Logan."

"My pleasure," my brother said with a schoolboy grin.

We both watched her walk away, Logan taking special care to check out her posterior in her tight skirt.

"This is gonna be fun. Don't you think? Just the Ryan boys wreaking havoc."

"What on earth are you doing here?" I asked, this time repeating my thought out loud.

"You aren't the only one who can manipulate."

"This isn't some game, Logan. You need to leave… now." I tried to keep my voice down, but the venom in my words wiped the grin from my brother's face.

"What gives?"

"Father chose me to bring the 'Second Alpha' back. Not you. Me."

"That was his first mistake."

I took a step closer. "What's that supposed to mean?"

"It's simple. You're weak. You can't do this. I, on the other hand, can."

"You may have brawn, but I've got brains. I'm also quite the handsome young man. You, little brother, leave much to be desired."

He growled. "You just wait, I'll be cleaning up your mess."

"Whatever you say. Now get the hell out of here."

"You can be a real ass sometimes."

"Yeah, I can. Now leave."

He shot me a glare that prickled the hairs on the back of my neck before he sauntered away.

Moments later, Annabelle walked from her car toward the entrance to school. Time to head to Mr. Sassaman's class. If she liked it or not, she was about to meet her future boyfriend. At least her appearance was easy on the eyes. Light hair, blue eyes, slender build. I could work with that. It would've sucked if she looked like a dog. I've had that misfortune in the past when tracking girls.

With a crack of my knuckles, I headed inside. I couldn't help the adrenaline that coursed through my body. I'd give Logan a little credit for being right. This was gonna be fun. After all, "deception" was my middle name.

In the bushes, I shook my head to chase away the memory. I didn't want it to go any further, to when I first spoke to Belles.

Such a coward. That was how I'd describe myself now. A coward.

I'd never been here before, to the Arethusa Fountain at Bushy Park. Actually, I'd never been to London before. But Annabelle had. She came with her family last year and talked about it for weeks afterwards.

A pit swelled in my stomach that I now used this knowledge against her.

Still, here I was... about to deceive her for a second time. Annabelle's strength impressed me. It also scared the shit out of me. I couldn't believe she'd gotten this far. Just yesterday she'd found the flower that'd unlock the door to the Lake of Elfin.

That's why I did this, I told myself for the millionth time. *I had to.*

I pushed aside a branch to better see her. She stood on the top tier of the Arethusa Fountain, her palm placed gently in Arethusa's stone hand, head down. Every piece of me wanted to look away, but I couldn't. The movement of her lips transfixed me and sent a chill throughout my body. It didn't matter that I couldn't hear her words. She spoke to a statue, searching for hope in any way she could.

This desperation pulled me from my hiding spot and toward the still water that encased the motionless fountain. As I walked, I brushed the dirt from my hands against my jeans.

"You're late," I called out, my breath lingering in the chilly air.

At first she didn't turn, but her hands shot open before balling into fists. I knew she recognized my voice. I couldn't read her thoughts, nor did I need to. I couldn't shake how her face had paled as I revealed myself on the beach the other day. When I pulled back my selkie skin to allow the moonlight to expose my human form.

Now bit-by-bit she faced me. Dark circles accompanied her eyes, a bruise budded on her chin, and her hair clung to her face from the earlier rain.

She still looked beautiful.

Her voice, on the other hand, spat at me with an uninviting tone. "Where's my sister?"

Tentatively, I raised my palms and took a step into the pool surrounding the fountain. She watched as I took one stride after another toward the first of the four tiers. If the white of her clenched knuckles was any indication, each step caused her anger to rise in intensity.

"I said, where's my sister? You sick bastard."

"Hey, now. Belles, let me explain."

"I don't want you to explain. I want you to tell me where Lindsey is."

"I'll make you a deal. Just listen. Then, I'll tell you where Lindsey is."

"No, Blake. That isn't how it's going to go. You're going to tell me where she is. And then we're going to leave."

"Sorry, Belles… but you're going to play by my rules this time."

I cringed as I watched the thoughts dance behind her eyes. I hated playing with her emotions. I knew how much her sister meant to her. I had no choice though. This acted as my last chance to make her understand.

"I'm waiting," I said, taking another step forward. "What's it going to be? Are you going to come down from there and listen? Or should I just leave?"

"Fine." She jumped down a level from where Arethusa stood and I quietly exhaled. "I'll give you five minutes. Then you need to keep up your end of the bargain."

I didn't think five minutes would be enough, but I'd take anything I could get. As she ascended from the fountain, my heart rate quickened. The last time I'd been this close to her, Kerberos had knocked my Belles unconscious on that beach.

Impulsively, I took another step.

"Don't come any closer," she warned.

I gestured at the stone base of the fountain. "Can I at least get out of the water?"

"Really, Blake? You're a seal for Christ's sake and you want to get out of the water?"

I couldn't help it, a sly smile crossed my lips. *Damn, I missed her.*

"You've always been quick-witted, Belles. I like that about you. You know what else I like?"

Her arms crossed. "What's that? The fact that you so easily duped me?"

"No. Everything."

Her face didn't reveal even the slightest gateway into her thoughts. "Great. I'm glad I'm so well liked. So what'd you want to tell me?"

"The truth."

That I never wanted to deceive you over the past year. Or even right now.

"Well that'll be something new."

Her words stung and I didn't want her to see my reaction. I quickly walked past her along the narrow ledge of the fountain. Like a dagger, a jolting pain plunged into my heart as she twisted her body to avoid any contact with me.

I faced her again, but only saw her back. Running my fingers through my shaggy brown hair, I spoke more to myself than to Belles. "I deserved that."

When she finally turned, defiance burned in her eyes. Even more so when she climbed another tier of the fountain, forcing me to look up to see her face.

Her confidence drove me to avert my eyes. Perhaps my shame added to it. Regardless, when I spoke, I concentrated on a wet footprint I'd left behind. "You know… I didn't know anything about you when they told me to befriend you."

Sarcasm oozed from her voice. "Well that changes everything, now doesn't it? Where's Lindsey?"

This time, I met her eyes. "It's not like I had a choice. I was raised in this dystopia. I was taught that the Tritons were power hungry. That the Guardians were merciless and would do whatever necessary to get the shell back."

"No, Blake. The Guardians protect innocent humans and sprites from people like you."

"I see that now. Because of you. But I didn't before. For as long as I can remember, it was drilled into my head that the Guardians had one focus: themselves. They didn't protect humans for the greater good; they protected humans so they'd remain undiscovered. So they could search for the shell and the 'Second Alpha' without humans getting in the way."

"Oh please, you guys searched for the 'Second Alpha' too. Except you killed people while doing so. The Guardians never did that."

I threw up my hands, but as if too heavy, they fell right back to my legs. "I know, Belles. You know when things changed for me?"

"Enlighten me."

"That night on the Ferris wheel. Do you remember what I said to you?"

"No."

It took all my strength not to crumble. That moment had meant the world to me. In fact, it became my downfall. I needed to make her remember. "I took your hand in mine and I said, 'I really like you.'"

I yearned to hear her thoughts, but she only turned her head adding another layer of torture to my torment. The movement exposed the small freckles that lined the right side of her neck. I always joked that they formed a heart, my heart.

She erased the symbol of love as she faced me. A little more of my heart broke. "Well, I should've known then that you're a liar. Would've saved me a lot of trouble."

"Okay, I'll admit it, when I first met you… I didn't care about you. You were just a job. And you weren't my first. I befriended a few girls before you."

Her head shook. "So you lured multiple girls into the water to drown them?"

My head shook, but for a different reason. "I never hurt anyone. I, um, led them there. But I didn't kill them. I swear."

"It's the same damn thing. Those people were innocent. Because of you they're dead. Just some 'job' to you."

"Trust me, I feel horrible about it."

"Trust you? Trust you? You must be kidding me. Why would I ever trust you?"

"You did at one time."

"I was wrong. Very, very wrong."

"I didn't have a choice. I know that sounds like a pathetic excuse, but it's true. When Alastor tells you to do something, you do it."

"Who the hell is that?" she demanded.

"He's our leader. An avenger of control. His bloodline is defiant against the Guardians who seek Triton's shell. He believes we shouldn't be domineered again. Anyone who disobeys him isn't met with mercy. You're seen as standing in the way of the betterment of our kind."

"That's a load of crap."

"Maybe so, but it's something taken very seriously. Especially for me."

"Why?"

"My father..." The great Oscar Ryan. "He's Alastor's second-in-command. Within the selkies, you answer to my father. I didn't have the easiest upbringing. I'm supposed to one day rule the selkies."

I'm supposed to be the great Blake Ryan, I thought with self-loathing.

Annabelle didn't respond, only stared. My hope that she recognized the situation I faced slipped away with her next question.

"Were you going to lure me into the water? Is that why you suggested we go to Atlantic City?"

I didn't want to answer her, but I needed her to see things through my eyes. Alastor had commanded me to lure her to the water. He wanted to know if she could breathe it. If she held the title of the "Second Alpha."

"I told you, things changed for me, Belles. That night at the festival, they changed. For months I struggled with my feelings versus my duty to Alastor."

"Just answer me," she demanded. "Is that why you wanted to see that concert?"

My eyes dropped in an attempt to avoid her accusatory eyes. "Yes." I paused for the cold air to fill my lungs. "They made me. I tried to fix it. When that guy showed up at the school, I tried to race to your house. I didn't know if you saw a Tracker or a Guardian. I wasn't sure if the others sensed my hesitation to capture you."

"You were there? At my house?"

"Yes, I saw the Guardian take you. I felt so helpless. And I tried to get you away from that merman when you were in the net."

"Wait, that was you? That insane tug-of-war?"

My cheeks burned with shame. "I lost. But I tried again. I swear."

"So it was you… chasing us in the caves?"

"No, that wasn't me. I wouldn't hurt you. They bragged about it. How you got banged up a little. It took all my willpower not to… I had to play along."

"Why? Why didn't you just leave?"

I looked intently into her eyes, hoping my words reached her. "So I could be on the inside and know what was going on. I wanted to protect you, to set things right."

"What do you mean?"

"Alastor is ruthless. After you escaped from the caves, he told us to kill you on sight. He didn't want me involved anymore, but I convinced my father to talk to him. When you came out of that alcove with the coins, I didn't steal them for my own benefit. I wanted you to follow me. I thought if you chased me to shore, I could explain everything. But the others followed."

She rubbed the back of her head where Kerberos had hit her. A look of pain seared across her face before she looked me again in the eyes, this time softer. "So what happened next?"

"I played along. I patted them on the back, told them job well done, and convinced them to take you and that merman back to headquarters instead of killing you. I wanted to make sure they didn't hurt you. Things got heated when we were debating on how to…

handle things. We all heard the commotion. Voices, doors slamming, and saw Nysa was missing."

"Who?"

"The young mermaid, the princess of Tritonis."

"Her name is Aurelia."

"Right, sorry. When Aurelia went missing and they followed after, I decided to leave once and for all." I left out the part how Alastor demanded that I stay behind. He no longer trusted me. "As you guys escaped, so did I."

"So all this time you were just trying to help me?"

"Yes, all I want is for you to be safe."

I knew the moment realization hit her. When my plan became transparent.

"Lindsey isn't here, is she?"

No, I thought to myself before I said it out loud.

The slight acceptance I'd seen in her eyes disappeared. "Where is Lindsey? Where is my sister?"

"I'd imagine she's safe and sound at home."

I meant for the words to be playful and relief washed over me as some of her anger disappeared. Instead, she just looked tired.

"Why?" she said. "Why did you bring me here?"

"They want you dead. There are plans to ambush you before you go to the Lake of Elfin. I'm not talking about just a few Trackers either. A war. I couldn't let it happen. I had to keep you away."

"So this isn't some ploy to stop me from getting to the shell and giving control back to the Tritons?"

Her words slapped me coldly across the face. For the third time, I looked away. My eyes found Arethusa above us.

"Come on, Blake. You can't be surprised I'm questioning your motives. You led me here under false pretenses, after lying to me about your real identity."

I whirled back around to face her, heat filling my voice. "I know! You don't think I see the suspicion and doubt in your eyes? It kills me. The worst thing is... I didn't ask for this. For any of it." My hands scrubbed through my hair in frustration. "You think I wanted to fall for you? To deceive you? To turn my back on the only family I've ever known because of my feelings for you? I've been living in this self-inflicted hell for the past year of my life."

For the first time, I think my words truly sunk in. She stood there motionless, except for the rise of her chest as she deeply inhaled.

"I need to go," she finally said.

"What?"

"I need to go. I have a duty to the sprites."

I hadn't meant for it, but anger bubbled into my voice. "You've got to be kidding me."

"What? No. I'm the 'Second Alpha,' Blake. As crazy as that sounds, I am. And I need to live up to the expectation of that title. I came here because I thought my sister was in danger. Trust me, it was a decision that tore me up inside. Now that I know she's safe, I need to go."

"You're going to leave? Just like that? And risk your life for them?"

"Yes."

"But what about us?" To me, Annabelle was still my girlfriend. She was mine. "Did nothing I just said change anything?"

"I don't know. I don't have the luxury of thinking about that right now."

"Stay with me. Please, just stay with me. Let the others fight this battle."

"I'm sorry. I can't."

That was when it hit me. That merman who helped her... I couldn't miss the worry in her eyes when I stole the coins from him. Collins had told me how she hesitated to leave him.

"It's because of him, isn't it?"

"Who?"

"You know who I'm talking about."

"Adrian?"

"Whatever his name is. Is he the reason you have to leave?"

Please say no, I thought as I closed my eyes.

"I don't know how to answer that question."

I should have stopped there. But I continued my self-destructive streak. The next question came out before I knew it.

"You're worried about him, aren't you?"

She threw up her hands. "Of course I am. He's my friend!"

"And is that all? Is he just your friend?"

"Blake. Look, I'm sorry, but I need to go. Can't you understand? You were willing to risk your life for me."

"But that's different. That's because I love you!"

Immediately, her eyes dropped to the ground while my hands clutched over my pounding heart. It was true. I had lost her to him. I yearned to disappear. To find the nearest dark spot and crawl into it.

I didn't think the situation could get any worse. I was wrong... very, very wrong.

My brother's voice added salt to my already exposed wound. "Well isn't this an awkward moment?"

He stood within the fountain's pool, only ten feet from us. I hadn't even registered his feet moving through the water. Venom all but spilled from my voice when I addressed him, "Logan, what are you doing here?"

"Aren't you happy to see me, brother?"

"Happy isn't a word I ever use to describe you."

"Now, now. There's no need to be mean. I just had to see this for myself. Father will be so proud."

"Go to Hell."

"Such a temper on this one. Don't you think, Annabelle?"

Just hearing him say her name made my battered feelings no longer matter. Instinctively, I stepped in front of her, blocking Annabelle from Logan. "Don't you dare talk to her."

"Or what, brother?"

"Don't test me."

Logan scoffed, staring intently at us. "Test you? Now why would I do that? You've already made your choice to betray us."

"You really shouldn't talk about things you know nothing of."

"Oh really?" he said as his brow rose. "Perhaps you could fill me in."

"You aren't worth the explanation."

He feigned a pout that turned into a sneer. "Now you've hurt my feelings."

"Why are you here, Logan?"

"That answer is simple enough. I came to finish what you've started."

Annabelle's body tensed behind me. I reached my arm behind to steady her. I think I had to touch her to steady myself as well. I needed it before I spoke. I prayed strength infused each word. "Let me be clear of one thing, *brother*. You will not lay a hand on Annabelle."

"Is that so? Father is quite disappointed in you. In fact, he's denounced you as his successor. It appears I now have that honor."

"It's not an honor," I snapped. "It's a disgrace."

Logan waved his hand at nothing. "Tomato, tom-ah-to. Now back to business. Are you going to hand her over? Or am I going to have to take her?"

"I think you know."

"I was hoping you'd say that. Do you know how long I've waited for this moment? To fight my big brother once and for all."

"I didn't realize you thought that fondly of me."

"Fondly? Not quite. But I am sick and tired of this illustrious way people see you. Frankly, it bores me."

I didn't have a response. He wasn't worth it.

His eyes narrowed, a reaction I assumed to my stoic stance. "Don't tell me you are that blind. That you don't bask in the glory that Father bestows on you. His perfect son. And what am I? Nothing.

Until now. You see, this is my chance to kill two birds with one stone. You and Annabelle. Oh, I've been waiting for this day for so long."

My body stiffened as I realized he spoke to Annabelle instead of me. I didn't understand his motivations. Honestly, it didn't matter. My mind worked on overdrive as I figured out a way to get my Belles to safety.

With a plan forming, I turned to brush my lips against her ear. "Go, Belles. Run. When you get to the edge of the fountain, use your fire affinity."

I wasn't sure if this affinity had developed or not. I hoped it had. Her response allowed me to exhale. "What? No, you'll be trapped inside."

"Don't worry about me. I just want you to be safe, happy. Even if that's not with me."

"Blake—"

"Go. Now."

"I can't just leave you!"

"Listen to me. You need to do what's right... and that's helping the sprites. I see that now. Take Crowe's Crossing."

Logan stepped closer, unhappy with our whispered exchange. "Now speak up you two. Didn't anyone tell you that secrets are no fun?"

Annabelle's rushed voice tore my attention back to her. "I don't know what you're talking about."

I half turned, keeping my eyes on my brother. "It connects the fresh water beneath the earth. Under the bridge, there's a trapdoor. It's the fastest way to get to the lake."

"Crowe's Crossing?" she asked, repeating the phrase.

"I've only heard of its existence."

"But—"

I barely acknowledged her response. Logan's eyes captivated me. The hatred boiled there before the muscles in his arms and legs quivered, and then he made his move.

He launched his nearly two-hundred pound frame at Annabelle. Logan moved fast, but so did I. In a heartbeat, I grabbed Annabelle and tossed her to the side. Then stride for stride I matched his steps, angling my approach to intercept his path toward my Belles.

Our collision stopped me like a violent wave. I may be older, but Logan's size outmatched mine.

I swung with my right arm, but he easily dodged it. As he stood up to his full height, he threw his fist into my stomach. My body doubled over in pain as his shoulders rammed into mine, knocking me backward into the knee-high water. He didn't ease up, his body landed on mine, his knuckles meeting my face. I managed to get in a blow as his attention shifted to Annabelle. But it was too late. My strike did nothing. I'd failed. He remained unfazed as he climbed off my body and toward her.

Annabelle now nearly reached the edge of the fountain. At a crawl, she pulled herself onto dry land.

Come on, I silently prodded.

Logan's strides cut through the water, closing the distance between them. As he neared, he leaned forward, ready to pounce. Before he could, Annabelle thrust her palms downward to meet the water.

Instantly, fire erupted.

The burst of flames shot into the sky, throwing Logan backward. He landed with a thud against the pool's bottom. The two feet of water did little to cushion his fall.

In the blink of an eye, the blaze took on a life of its own, spreading along the perimeter of the water's surface until a full circle closed around us.

My head swiveled in all directions. The power that Annabelle yielded inside of her astonished me.

Why did it take me so long to realize the life I led was wrong? If I hadn't, perhaps she'd still be mine.

Logan's movements across the pool pulled my attention back to the here and now. I scurried to my feet to prepare for his next attack. As he stepped forward, I matched with a backward stride. My soaked hair dripped, leaving streaks down my bloodied face and disappearing into the rough water at my feet.

"Look what you've done now," he said with a growl, as if in his selkie form.

"Yes, brother, let's look at what I've done. Annabelle is off to retrieve Triton's shell from the lake."

"She doesn't stand a chance."

"We'll see about that."

Disbelief filled his eyes as he edged closer. "You really chose to turn against us because of some girl?"

I wanted to hate my brother, but as I continued to match his movements, I pitied him. He'd never experienced love. Our father emanated coldness. His interactions with us consisted of training, scheming, and what I now recognized as brainwashing. And our mother. Our mother had been the only compassion and grace in my life. But never in Logan's. She sacrificed her life for his. My young age left me unaware at the time, but tales from the day told me the physicians warned her that the risk of childbirth was severe. Still, she pleaded with the doctors to put Logan's wellbeing before her own.

Selkies deliver in their human form, but the baby looks like a tiny seal. Our father was there to embrace Logan as he entered the world but he quickly tore his hands away after my mom's eyes fluttered closed.

But that wasn't what transformed my father into a hateful sprite. From what I remembered, he'd always been that way. Over the years, I wondered how someone like my mother could love someone like him. Perhaps the saying held truth, love was blind.

Annabelle couldn't see the evil that lurked behind my façade. The difference between the dynamic of my parents and Annabelle and me was that I wanted to change for her. That realization acted as the catalyst to disown myself as my father's son. To abjure myself from the Trackers.

The need to tell my brother as much rushed from my lips.

"Fine by me," he snarled. "Father has already disowned you anyway. Do you not remember the part where I told you that I'm next in line to rule the selkies?"

"Logan, you don't need to follow in his footsteps."

"I don't *need* to? That's okay. I want to."

His pace quickened and I raised my hands in a defensive stance. Like a boxer in a ring, he circled around me. A malevolent smile crossed his lips as his head bobbed from side to side, trying to juke me.

One arm then another jabbed at me, even though he wasn't within reach.

"I can do this all night, Blake."

I knew he could, and that worried me. He moved. I moved. Each backward motion I made brought me closer to the wall of fire. The wetness on my brow from the water mixed with sweat from my movements and also the flickering flames. The flames nearest to Blake continued at full blaze.

"What's your plan here?" I asked him as I eyed the fire to my left and formed my own. The sounds of distant voices mixed with the crackling sounds of the reds, oranges, and blues.

"Well, I figured I'd take care of you and then go after your girlfriend. This fire can't last forever."

I bared my own teeth in response.

He playfully slapped his hand to his forehead. "Silly me, I meant to say your ex-girlfriend."

Something deep inside me snapped. I charged at Logan, catching him off guard. My shoulders barreled into his stomach as my arms wrapped around his torso. Together we tumbled back into the water.

I didn't let Logan suck in any air before I thrust him below the water's surface. His legs kicked wildly and his arms pummeled into my sides, but I didn't feel each blow. I saw red. I only thought of Annabelle.

In the end, these thoughts loosened my hold before I did something I'd regret for the rest of my life. Exhausted, I rolled off my brother and pushed to my feet. More than anything, Logan's ego would be bruised and I didn't have long before he also stood six feet tall.

With the plan that took form just a few moments ago pulsating in my head, I trudged through the water toward the wall of fire. The heat radiated into my body as I neared. But that wasn't all that happened. The flames once again flickered.

My Belles is a clever girl, I thought as I inwardly smiled.

She controlled her affinity with her mind. Mine told me that she worded her command in such a way that only Logan would be trapped inside.

I'd denounced my brother, my father, the Trackers, my way of life. I didn't know her exact thoughts, but I imagined my disownment now allowed me to escape her ring of fire.

The sound of angry water pulled my attention behind me to find Logan not only on his feet but also rushing at me. I prayed my assumptions and faith in Annabelle didn't prove me wrong as I rocked forward then backward on the balls of my feet.

On the count of three, I fought through the fatigue in my legs and leapt away from Arethusa and my brother. The heat of the fire left a momentarily chill on my body as I landed hard on the pavement.

Swarms of people reacted to my sudden appearance, shouting and running toward me. My eyes remained trained on the spot where I escaped the fountain, waiting to see if Logan's malevolent face would appear.

A firm hand on my shoulder ripped my attention away from the sea of flames.

"Are you okay, mate?" I heard, but didn't offer a response. The man shifted his gaze to the fire, when he turned back I'd already gotten to my feet. I spared one more glance in the direction of my brother's pyre cage then broke into a full sprint. The sounds of an approaching fire engine fueled more adrenaline into my tired body.

At first my destination wasn't quite clear to me. I'd taken two trains to get to London from the water, and mostly because it was too early to find a cab. Now, a number of taxis had stopped to witness the oddity Annabelle had caused in Bushy Park. I threw open the door of one and jumped inside.

"English Channel!" I called to the driver.

He looked at me with wide eyes, just like the handful of people I passed as I sprinted away from Arethusa's fountain.

The confusion across his face increased with his response. "Could you give me something more specific?"

"Brighton Pier."

With a nod, the driver put the car into drive.

It'd take more than an hour to get to the water's edge. Thankfully, it was still early, on a holiday. My mind barely registered as we drove past the Hampton Court Palace. But as we passed over the Thames, my eyes scoured below the bridge and into the slow current for any sign of Annabelle. A crowd of men stood along the banister and also peered into the water, only looking up to exchange words and expressions. I smiled knowingly. Chances were they'd just witnessed her entrance into the river and now stood there mystified as to what the hell had happened. I hoped she'd find her way to the lake. I couldn't imagine that merman, Adrian, not having a plan.

The remainder of my ride to the pier passed uneventfully. On occasion, the driver eyed me curiously in the rear view mirror. His gaze lingered on my swollen cheekbone, but he never spoke a word. The radio was turned off, and the silence left me uneasy. The folds of my mind kept trying to resurface thoughts of Annabelle and of my past, but I pushed each one away.

My chest dramatically rose and fell as the cab eventually pulled up alongside the curb at Brighton Pier. As I hopped out, I gave him way too big of a tip.

As nonchalantly as possible, I waited for the cabbie to drive away before I bypassed the entrance to the pier and descended to the sand beneath. Confetti and empty bottles littered the ground from the New Year's Eve celebrations the night before. I didn't waste any time. With my back flush against the wood of the pier, I counted four steps forward, one step to the right, and six steps to the left. The same numbers that made up my birthday, April sixteenth.

There, I sunk to my knees and pawed at the sand, creating a discarded pile to my side. Before I knew it, I caught sight of the gray colored skin of my pelt. As I kicked the dirt back into the hole, I shook out my sealskin of excess sand. I was about to step into it when another thought danced across my mind.

Logan may have said the fire can't last forever, but I had another solution to stop him from hurting Belles. He had followed me to London. His own pelt must be close by.

My father may have taught us how to fight, but as a big brother I taught him the ins and outs of being a selkie. We revered our skin, especially after it left our body. Without it, we couldn't return to our non-human form. Every selkie had their own system of hiding their pelt on land. Like an ATM code, you don't share it with others. Except for maybe family. Only Logan knew my method of safeguarding my skin.

I jogged back to the pier's column and walked seven paces forward, turned to my right but didn't move, then took two steps to my left. July second.

As I suspected, I soon held my brother's sacred sealskin. Carrying both, I walked to where the waves crashed onto the shore. There, I shook out my skin once more then stepped into it like a potato sack. As I pulled it up my body, my legs fused together, the pelt melted into my skin, and my fat thickened. I threw my arms though the "sleeves" then wiggled my body to cover my head. As soon as each portion touched my human-like form, I transformed until I resembled a gray seal. The process didn't hurt at all. Quite seamless, actually. For selkies, all that remained from our human form were our eyes. My big brown ones quickly found Logan's skin and secured it between my teeth.

With the help of the surf, I padded deeper into the English Channel.

Goodbye, brother, I thought as I kicked my tail and dove through a crashing wave.

But I knew this wasn't goodbye, not for real. Logan would forever haunt my memories and act as a reminder of the evil that once lurked deep inside. For now, I forced myself to concentrate on the situation at hand.

Unfortunately, taking the jet streams wasn't a possibility. It'd save time, but the danger of being spotted inside was high. I knew the other Trackers would be thrilled to get their hands on me. Most likely, a command that came from my father. The shadows of the open sea provided better protection. Besides, selkies preferred to avoid jet streams. They only quickened our pace moderately and the stream created a tight fit as we shot through the water.

At this point in time, my main concern centered on helping Belles. I couldn't venture into the fresh water lake, but I could shift into my human form to get to its banks. In the end, I decided against going back on land. My goal consisted of the waters of the Bristol Channel. That was where the Trackers hoped to intercept Annabelle.

I swam all afternoon and into the night with Logan's pelt in tow. I knew it must have gotten late, rather it was now the very early hours of the next day. Then I saw them. Not just the Trackers but also the Guardians. Off in the distance, a war had broken out at the base of an underwater mountain where the sea met the channel. Hundreds of sprites faced off, the clanking noises of sword hitting sword traveled through the water to meet me. I quickened my pace to reach the outskirts of the battle. But as I neared, I slowed, dropping my brother's pelt. I didn't watch as it slipped into the depths of the sea beneath me.

I no longer pledged my allegiance to the Trackers. Yet I also had no ties to the Guardians. For the first time in my life, I was a nomad. My loyalties fell only to one person, to Annabelle. Although I couldn't think of her as mine anymore, I decided to help the Guardians. At full speed, I flew into the side of an unsuspecting Tracker. The Guardian he battled quickly swung his sword down, making contact with his body.

In that moment, the Guardian and I made eye contact. His hand hesitated to raise his blade again, confusion clouding his face. I didn't provide him the opportunity to decide my fate. I swam off in a flash to my next victim. With a twist of my body, I whacked another Tracker with my tail. Just as quickly, I dodged another Tracker's sword.

In battle, selkies weren't the best suited. We didn't yield a sword, a gun, or anything else of that sort. Our advantages rested on the use of our bodies. Oftentimes, we were called upon to help shield a merman, for our speed, or our brute force. While trying to evade the weapons of the Trackers, I tried to harness these strengths.

Suddenly, a slight pulse of a current rocked me. The Tracker just feet away went still in the water as the flow wrapped around his body. The Guardian quickly reacted, swiping the sword across his throat. A moment later, the current dropped, allowing the Tracker's lifeless body to sink.

Only one sprite had the ability to control water in such a way. A mixture of butterflies and also dread filled my insides. Turning my head, I spotted her. Annabelle descended along the side of the mountain toward the battle with an outstretched hand. One by one, she picked out a Tracker as the next victim of her water affinity. In her other hand, she held Triton's shell.

I don't know why it came as a surprise that she'd retrieved the conch shell from the Lake of Elfin, but it did. Now she was here. In the very place that I wanted to keep her from. That thought acted as blinders as I fought my way across the battlefield, the need to protect her fueling each movement.

That was when it happened: the Tracker pulled back his arm as I closed the distance to Annabelle. As he released the spear, time slowed down. Her eyes remained trained on something across the battlefield, unaware of the fatal blow aimed at her. I kicked my tail with a ferocity that launched me forward, my head making contact with her ribs. Instantly, pain seared through my underbelly.

Blood leaked from my stomach, but my attention remained on Annabelle. The shell that had flown from her hands held her focus. She dove then wrapped her fingers around the shell as she seamlessly brought it to her lips. Her chest rose as she gathered air then released it into Triton's shell.

Even though I'd abjured my kind, I expected the current to whisk me away. That was its purpose… to stop a Tracker's attack. Instead, I watched as the current hit the Tracker army like a wave, leaving me untouched. Then as if a giant net swooped down, the current ripped each and every malevolent sprite away until their bodies disappeared.

I allowed my eyes to close. Not just from the pain of the spear, but also because Annabelle was safe. The Trackers were gone. My attempts to keep her away from the battle with a fake ransom note didn't work, but my success came by intercepting the deadly weapon meant to take her life.

A touch near my wound caused my eyes to jump open. She looked like an angel. Concern created every crease across her forehead. As her blue eyes drifted to meet my brown, her face took on a look of recognition before concern once again washed over her.

This time, Annabelle's hand rested on the side of my head and I leaned into her touch.

"You saved me…" she whispered with a tremble in her voice.

In that moment, I realized that everything had been worth it. All the self-inflicted hatred and spitefulness brought me to this exact place in time. I'd become the person that Annabelle thought me to be all along.

It gave me renewed strength.

"I don't believe you can avoid your fate. Nor do I think you can change it. The real challenge is recognizing when you've achieved it."

- Blake

AN ANTHOLOGY

Lady Katherine

As I pulled open the door to my dormitory building at UCLA, I reveled at how much my life had changed. I now wore shoes, my hair hung dry in loose curls, and denim covered my legs. Such simple things, yet I'd never worn this type of clothing before. Just nine months ago the prophecy kept me and the other fae trapped within the Lake of Elfin.

Yes, Elfin constituted a remarkable place to live. There I wed the fae of my dreams. James carried the title of Lord: the next in line to rule the water fairies of my home. At his side, I'd one day be his queen. That wasn't what made Elfin so desirable though. The combination of the sprites that dwelled there, the connection we maintained with the earth, our eloquent town, and the fair rule of my father-in-law, King James III, manifested a peaceful environment.

Still, I yearned to know what existed beyond our realm. The island in the middle of the Lake of Elfin formed the only dry land my feet had ever touched. The ground held bountiful beauty. Thousands and thousands of years ago, this led to our downfall when the "First Alpha" stole the precious Columnea Billbergia flower from the gardens before slipping through our trapdoor. From that point on, it remained locked, allowing no one to pass through.

I had dreamed for the prophecy to be fulfilled during my lifetime. Still, surprise washed over my body on that eve when Annabelle graced us with her presence. The manner in which she did so no longer held importance. For her actions, I presented her with my sincere gratitude.

And now we fostered a great friendship, even sharing a dormitory room. She referred to me as Katie, the only one who sought not to call me by my given name. I spoke hers as Onnabelle. The only one who softened her Christian name. I believed the hard sound of the "A" clashed with the delicate nature of her heart.

I smiled as I eyed the stark white walls and bright-papered flyers that occupied any empty space. One spoke of a "Back to School Bash." I hadn't yet attended any human celebrations, but our academic year had only begun a few weeks prior. Like Annabelle, my studies revolved around medicine. I craved to further my bond with the earth.

As I turned the corner to my hall, my head cocked to the side. A dashing young man knocked at our door. A moment later, Annabelle answered it. I knew it rude to interrupt so I held my place. I also found it rude to eavesdrop, but I simply couldn't help myself.

I watched as Annabelle took a step back, disappearing from my view. Her voice carried toward me still. "What are you doing here?"

"Um, I go here," the boy replied with a playful grin.

"What?"

"Yes, Belles. We were both accepted. Remember?"

"But—"

"But you thought I wasn't going to come after… everything that happened."

From my position down the hall, no words carried to reach me. Instead, her gentleman caller spoke again. "Didn't Prince Adrian tell you?"

"Tell me what?"

"I'm one of them now. A Guardian."

Her voice filled with distress. "No. No, he didn't tell me that."

I watched as the boy's grin widened. "Makes sense, I guess."

"What does?"

"That he didn't tell you."

"And why is that?"

"Looks like Prince Adrian is afraid of a little competition."

With that, he shrugged and turned down the hall toward me.

With a jolt, I tried to busy myself with the dormitory rules posted on the wall. The door clicked closed, but I didn't risk a glance.

The thudding of his footsteps against the flooring neared. As he passed, he spoke to my back, "Good morning, Lady Katherine."

With an open mouth, I watched as he strutted away.

And who might you be?

As soon as he disappeared around the corner, I turned on my heels with swiftness.

A lady never practices haste, I reminded myself as I mindfully walked toward my room.

The last few strides weren't as graceful, and neither were my quick-handed taps against the door. I hadn't any time to find my keys within my bag.

At the same time, Annabelle swung the door open and bellowed into my face, "What now?"

Upon seeing me, her hand dropped from the knob. "Oh, Katie. It's you. Sorry."

My roommate had quite the flare for the dramatics. Turning away from the door she flung herself across her bed, burying her face amidst a pillow.

I quietly pressed the door closed before settling on her bedside. "What's caused you such sorrow?"

In response, her shoulders trembled. I closed my eyes, fearful I'd added to her grief. But when I opened them, Annabelle faced me, laughter slipping from her lips.

"The way you form each thought gets me every time."

I suppose I had a proper tongue. Annabelle expressed amusement on more than one occasion over the past few weeks. I returned her smile, pleased to see suffering hadn't caused the quiver in her shoulders.

Now that she sat at ease, I pushed again for her to divulge the identity of that boy. "I'm still waiting, Annabelle."

She sat up, crossing her legs. "Well, that was Blake. My boyfriend turned ex-boyfriend. The one who was really a Tracker, but later saved my life."

Recognition passed over my face. I'd heard all about him and Annabelle's trials and tribulations from months ago. "So what are you going to do?"

"I have no clue. I'm with Adrian. I love Adrian. To be honest, I haven't allowed myself to think about Blake since that day."

"But you once cared deeply for him?"

She sighed. "Yes. My first love. And I'm over it... the whole him lying to me thing. It's obvious he's changed."

Annabelle's first love hoped she believed this to be true. Over the next few weeks, he courted her. Each day he called upon her. But each night she slipped into the depths of the LA River and ventured toward the marina where Prince Adrian waited. Because of her devotion to Prince Adrian, she refused Blake's early advances. Finally, she succumbed to Blake's charm and agreed to accompany him one eve.

The whole evening my husband played in jest with me that he should've visited at another time. Apparently, Annabelle's love life left me quite enamored. One time I even turned to James and whispered, "I cannot wait until her return."

His gentle laugher filled the room and I sunk deeper into his embrace. I cherished his holidays with me when he came to visit. Our separation left me doubting my decision to explore the outside world. Each time I expressed my concerns, his fingers trailed lightly down my face and he offered a reassuring word.

We spent our evening sharing tales of our recent days, but also flipping the web and surfing the channels on the TV. Phrases I hoped I'd delivered in the correct manner. The Internet and television shows fascinated us both. I'd grown accustomed to them. James hadn't yet much exposure. I'd barreled over with laughter each time he believed the actor on screen to be directing his words at him.

Safely tucked within James' arms, my eyes had just drifted closed when a key slipped into the lock. Instantly, I bolted upright.

"No longer so tired, my love?" James questioned as he turned on a light. He loved doing so, as electricity held great attraction for him.

I gave him a smile as Annabelle opened the door, allowing for me to catch a peep of Blake. He stood there in jeans and a T-shirt beaming with what Annabelle had previously described as his "oh-so-sexy" grin.

A look of contentedness but also something else simmered on her face as she closed the door at her back and slipped into the room.

"Spill it," I demanded, using a phrase I'd learned.

She dropped onto her bed across from mine. "I'm confused," she pouted.

"Well, go on," I encouraged. "Commence from the beginning."

"You really want to hear all this?"

"Please," James said. "Do not allow her to beg."

He squeezed my arm as I laughed. "I will. It's not beneath me."

I was the ever-engaged audience as Annabelle shared her evening's details with us.

"We did something Adrian and I'd never be able to do together," she said. "It makes me wonder if he chose it on purpose."

Before she continued, I insisted she tell me all about bowling. Naturally, I'd never done it before but James assured me that we'd do so in the morrow. The idea of renting shoes simply enthralled me seeing as I'd been barefoot in my years thus far.

"It was like we picked up where we'd left off. Things just felt so natural." Annabelle said.

I leaned forward. "Please, tell me more."

"I expected it to be weird, but it wasn't. I mean, the last time I saw him was on the battlefield. Before that, he came clean about everything at the fountain."

"You hold faith in his words?"

"Yeah. He deceived me, but I still think there was truth in the year we shared together. At least parts of it. I tried to bring it up tonight, but his fingertip touched the freckles on my neck. He asked if we could leave it all in the past. It was such a familiar thing for him to do… to brush his hand across these marks. Honestly, it just reminded me of the past and how happy I'd been with him." Annabelle brushed her own fingers across her neck, then shook her head. "Blake always said my freckles formed a heart."

"Quite the romantic, is he not?"

She smiled. "I suppose, but so is Adrian."

Part of me considered it selfish to pull Annabelle from her current thoughts, but I desired more from her story. After bowling, Blake had provided the recommendation for ice cream. I'd had it just the other day and it delighted my palate. Although I fear most melted before I'd the opportunity to fully enjoy it.

"We sat on this bench right next to the shop," she said. "Catching up and stuff. He told me about his classes, his training as a Guardian, and also how he'd enrolled in ROTC, the Reserve Officers Training Corps.

"His drive impressed me. I always knew I wanted to be a doctor, but back in high school, Blake had no clue what he wanted to study. It made sense now, considering he thought he'd rule the selkies.

"But anyways, as we sat there he reached over and took my hand. The setting was perfect. Part of me screamed inside that it was wrong because of Adrian. The other part melted. My heart pounded so loud in my chest I hoped he couldn't hear it. When I looked over at him, he looked just as nervous. Somehow, that made holding his hand feel okay."

"Well, what came next?"

She fell back into bed and covered her face with her arms. "Then he walked me home." Her voice remained muffled as she spoke. "When we got to the door he asked me if he could see me again. I just stood there like an idiot."

"And?"

Propelling herself back to a sitting position, Annabelle twisted her bottom lip. "I said, 'sure.'"

I squealed and James playfully shook his head. "Dear Katherine, mind your manners."

I just as playfully struck him on his arm before regaining my composure. "Annabelle, the pressing question remains… what shall you tell Prince Adrian?"

"I don't know. I mean, Blake is just a friend. Nothing happened and I won't allow anything to happen."

I shot her a look with raised brows.

"Whatever, holding hands doesn't count," she insisted.

I'm not sure why Annabelle's love triangle provided me such pleasure. Perhaps it rested on the fact that James and I had been betrothed from a young age. I hadn't known anything different, nor did I seek it. Even if our parents hadn't arranged our marriage, I'd have hoped he'd one day court me. His strong face contrasted perfectly with his soft heart. To steal from human jargon, he was a ten. Simply laying eyes on him sent a flutter throughout my bones.

I recognized the same look in Annabelle's eyes when she returned home from a weekend holiday with Prince Adrian.

Without her knowledge, he'd created a sanctuary for them to together enjoy. Somewhere he'd hoped would ease the strain she carried in her shoulders. In the depths of the Pacific Ocean, he fashioned a retreat within a cave. A concealed fire created warmth and provided a soft glow. Soft blankets woven from seaweed allowed them to snuggle closely and share a comforting embrace. Lobster and king crab chased away hunger whenever it called. Mostly, they fell deep into each other's presence. Laughter, teasing, and soft touches formed an intimacy to forever hold in their hearts.

Her face held smooth lines upon her return. I fear as soon as Blake's name left my lips, those lines burrowed deeper along her brow. I regret how she looked at me with such sorrow when I proclaimed that she must choose between her suitors.

Much impressed me about my Annabelle. I deemed her pure of heart but her mind also held a sharpness I so desired. Amusement passed over me each morning and night. The thought would never have crossed my mind to make a list, but that was Annabelle. She summoned it her "pros and cons" to aid in her decision.

She'd practically float through the doors after an evening with Prince Adrian and jot down a note. After a day of bliss, a smile carried her back to that same paper to address a quality of Blake. I didn't envy her or her thoughts.

I allowed her to do so for a month, and then I sat her down. I clasped her hands in my own and looked into her pretty blue eyes. "The time has come, who's won your heart?"

She looked down at her list before pushing it aside. I smiled, knowing she'd speak earnestly and not from her note taking.

She took a deep breath, and then the words poured out. "Adrian is a really good kisser, although I haven't kissed Blake in a long time. I do remember him being good though. The type of kiss that made me forget my name.

"Blake and I had this intense passion for each other, but I also feel that same sensation with Adrian.

"I'd been with Blake for a year, but now Adrian and I've also been together for just as long.

"Blake makes me laugh so hard, but Adrian is also funny. Just in a different type of way.

"Adrian has this rugged type of handsomeness. The gods could've chiseled his face. Then there's Blake with this boyish charm.

"That's not to say that Adrian isn't playful. He is. He's got this jovial nature that I adore.

"Blake is protective and Adrian guards my heart.

"Adrian is well-educated. Not to say that Blake isn't smart.

"Blake is a born leader, but so is Adrian. I mean, Adrian will be king some day and he already calls me his queen.

"But he'll rule over the merfolk, which means a life in the sea. Blake can live up here. That means a life with my parents and Lindsey.

"I can obviously still see my family if I choose Adrian, but it'd mean time apart. It'd also mean time with Aurelia, Natasha, and YaYa. They're my family now, too.

"And yes, Blake can go in the water, but there he's a seal. Does that make up for the fact that Adrian can't ever go on land?"

She took a deep breath before locking eyes with me again. Confusion all but vibrated from her body as she clutched the necklace around her neck.

"Adrian is a gentleman, Blake is sweet.

"Adrian sacrificed our mission for me, Blake sacrificed his family for me.

"It'd rip my heart in two to break up with Adrian. But it wouldn't be any better to tell Blake that I couldn't see him anymore.

"Adrian and I have this connection where I feel like he reads my mind.

"Blake carries this intense confidence that somehow makes me feel more self-assured.

"Memories haunt Adrian that pull him from his sleep, but Blake has this darkness from his past that goes really deep.

"My parents already adore Blake and I haven't yet told them about Adrian. After my mom woke up from her surprise, I'm sure she'd love him though.

"To make things even more complicated, Adrian told me that he's dreamed of me all his life. Then there's Blake who risked everything to be with me.

"Adrian has this way of making any moment special.

"Blake creates these memories that I don't ever want to let go.

"They're both extremely supportive.

"They're both easy on the eyes.

"They both have a smile that warms me deep inside.

"In the end, they both want what's best for me."

She paused and I squeezed her hands. "Annabelle, who do you choose?"

"Can't I have both?"

"No, my dear. Who shall it be?"

She took another deep breath, closing her eyes. When she opened them once more, I knew her heart had settled on one.

"Adrian," she whispered.

"Fate is a funny thing. It has the power to bring you to a new world. Right where you feel you were meant to be in that moment in time."

- Lady Katherine

ABOUT THE AUTHOR

Leigh Michael is an author of YA fiction. Leigh was born and raised in the Philadelphia area where she attended Villanova University. It's here she decided to pursue a career in copywriting. Since then, Leigh has worked within the advertising world for nearly a decade before writing her debut series, Annabelle's Story.

Buy *Annabelle's Story* on Amazon and Barnes and Noble.

Learn more about Leigh and her books at
www.LeighMichaelBooks.com.
Follow Leigh on Twitter @LMichaelBooks
Like Leigh at Facebook.com/LeighMichaelBooks

AN ANTHOLOGY

Made in the USA
Charleston, SC
11 December 2012